Death on Cozumel Island

A CLAIRE O'KEEFE MYSTERY

CINDY QUAYLE

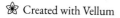 Created with Vellum

Chapter One

The steam rose from the carafe that held the dark amber liquid. I poured myself a cup of the fragrant brew and sat down on a chair.

Yum! This is heaven. I took a few more sips of the cardamon-infused coffee and looked around the small but ornately furnished apartment in Manama, Bahrain. It was like living in a movie set.

When I arrived in the capital of the small island country in the Persian Gulf six months ago, the university informed me that this beautiful apartment was part of my teaching benefits. I was also pleasantly surprised the school sent someone to meet me at the airport. I smiled recalling the verbal history lesson the university's representative, Ms. Nadia Al Moussa, gave me along the drive.

"Bahrain was believed to be part of the ancient Dilmun civilization...," Ms. Al Moussa recited as she pointed to the different landmarks as I looked out the car window. The traditional buildings were nestled between the modern skyscrapers with their glass walls and steel structures. The mix of modern and ancient architecture was stunning as was the setting sun that cast a warm glow on the city.

I also remembered feeling uneasy seeing the high stucco walls that surrounded a gated compound. However, Ms. Al Moussa put me at ease by explaining that the university housed the international faculty in these small, gated apartment homes. This made me feel better about living there alone.

Ms. Al Moussa also mentioned that having a gated residence was considered a status symbol for many people in Manama. I was impressed by the information. I doubted many of my colleagues were given homes with security systems.

Now over halfway through my one-year contract, I was torn about whether I wanted to extend my teaching job for another year. On one hand, the pay was great, and the faculty and students were wonderful to work with. On the other hand, I felt the irresistible itch to travel and live in new places.

I decided to push my indecision and call my best friend, Julia Kim. I picked up my phone and scrolled through my contacts. When I found Julia's number, I tapped the call button. It didn't take long before she answered my FaceTime call.

"Hi, Julia!" I said as my friend appeared on the screen. Even though her long black hair was pulled into a tight ponytail, and she was wearing a gray hoodie, she still looked cute.

"Hey, how are you doing?" Julia asked. Her face lit up in a big smile when she saw me.

"I'm good. I can't believe you're getting married in four months." I immediately brought up the topic Julia and I had been discussing nonstop over the past few weeks. I knew Julia was excited to get married, but she was overwhelmed with the wedding plans.

"I can't either. It feels like everything is happening so fast!" Julia groaned. She frowned as she scanned the wedding planning list. She held up the paper in front of the screen. "Look at this!"

The lined paper had small boxes next to phrases like *cake*

tasting and *party favors*. More boxes were not checked off than there were boxes that were marked.

"When are you coming to San Francisco? I could really use your help crossing off a lot of things on my list." Julia's eyebrows were furrowed.

"My last day of teaching at the university is December 23rd, and I'll fly out on the 25th," I said, sticking my tongue out in disgust. I wasn't thrilled that I had to fly on Christmas, but it was the cheapest airfare ticket.

"Have you thought about what you wanted to do for your bachelorette party?"

"What?" yelled Julia at her phone screen. "I can't hear you!" What's that noise in the background?" Our video call was interrupted by a sudden blaring in Arabic.

Without looking outside my apartment, I knew what was happening. I grinned at my best friend and said, "That's the call to prayer." The call to evening prayer was being broadcasted from a nearby mosque, and it was so loud that people couldn't ignore the call.

Although the volume was jarring for the first few weeks when I moved into my apartment, I had gotten used to the call of prayer. According to Islamic custom, every Muslim must pray five times a day. Therefore, the call to prayer was played over a loudspeaker five times a day, every day. This might seem excessive for many Westerners, but I didn't find it difficult to work around the prayer schedule.I just wished that the call to prayer wasn't so loud.

Since neither one of us could hear each other, Julia and I suspended our conversation. She brought her phone over to her Jack Russell Terrier, Grumpy, so I could see the adorable sleeping dog.

Julia adopted him from a local shelter while she was still in graduate school in Seattle. All of Julia's friends teased her about adopting Grumpy because she always said she didn't want a dog.

When she went to the shelter, she spotted an attendant holding a small ball of black and white fur which turned out to be Grumpy.

The attendant told her Grumpy was available for adoption, and if she knew anyone else who wanted to adopt puppies, the shelter was going to bring in four more Jack Russell Terrier puppies later that day. The owner of the dogs passed away unexpectedly leaving the four little puppies to fend for themselves until a neighbor walking her dog heard the cries. After hearing the sad story, Julia knew she had to adopt Grumpy and not a cat as she had originally intended to get.

I was so happy when Julia adopted a dog because I had always wanted one. Whenever I went to Julia in San Francisco, I spoiled the little pup with treats from the countries that I lived in. Julia joked Grumpy received better gifts than she did. I laughed and denied it when Julia made those remarks, but secretly, I knew Julia's statements were true. After several minutes of making kissy faces at Grumpy on the phone, the sound of the broadcast ended, signaling that everyone was inside the mosque.

"As I was saying before, what do you want to do for your bachelorette party?" I asked, picking back up on our conversation.

"Well," Julia said thoughtfully, "I was thinking I would like to do a destination bachelorette party."

My ears perked up when I heard the word *destination*. "Where were you thinking?" I tried to make my voice sound nonchalant, but my heart started to race, and my facial expression betrayed my excitement thinking about going someplace tropical.

Julia scrunched up her pretty face as she thought about where she wanted to go, and after a few seconds, her eyes lit up as she came up with a location. "I've got it. Let's go to Chicago!"

"What! In January? You want to have your bachelorette

party in one of the coldest and windiest cities in the U.S.?" I yelled. Chicago was not an answer I expected to hear.

"Why not? There are plenty of things to do in Chicago and not to mention some fantastic restaurants," Julia said logically.

My heart flopped at my friend's rational answers. "Okay." I tried to keep my face from showing my disappointment.

"I'm surprised you agreed so quickly," Julia said as she watched me intently. "I thought you would advocate for some-place warm like the Bahamas or Mexico."

"Uh... it is your party, and you know I'll go wherever you want," I said faithfully, but I was frazzled that Julia wanted to go to one of the windiest places in the United States during the winter. I debated whether I could change my friend's mind about the destination of her bachelorette party when her eyes twinkled, and she smiled.

"What?" I asked. I wondered if she changed her mind to someplace even colder than Chicago.

Julia couldn't keep up the charade and started to giggle. "I give up!"

"On what?" I was baffled by my friend's abrupt turn in the conversation. By now, Julia was clutching her stomach and laughing hysterically. So much so, the video of my friend was shaking.

"You should see your face!" Julia chortled into her phone. "I was just kidding about going to Chicago. You know I hate cold places just as much as you do."

"So, if you don't want to go to Chicago, then where do you want to go for your bachelorette party?" I asked Julia a little hesi-tantly because I wasn't convinced my friend hadn't lost it. I also silently thanked my lucky stars Julia was just kidding about going to Chicago. I had only been to Chicago once during the summer, and it was hot and humid. I could only imagine the extreme opposite if we visited the city in the middle of the winter. Thinking about the freezing temperature made me shiver!

"What about Cozumel?" Julia asked. "Do you remember how much we loved the island when we went there for our open-water certification dives in college?"

I sat up straighter. "Of course! How could I forget the blue, clear, and WARM waters of the Caribbean Sea?" Who was Julia kidding?

"The first time I dove underwater with all the sea life made me realize scuba diving was for me," I said. I also remembered Julia wasn't as thrilled as I was with our diving experience. Julia told me after we got certified she didn't want to go diving again because the diving gear was too cumbersome, and swimming against the current was exhausting.

"I'd love to go back to Cozumel, but I thought you didn't like it the last time we were there," I said warily not bringing up the past events. Even though I started to feel excited about going to Cozumel, I didn't want to get my hopes up because Julia could change her mind thinking about her dreadful time lugging the scuba gear and the rental air tanks.

"That's because I was there to get my scuba diving certification, and it wasn't as much fun for me as it was for you," Julia acknowledged. "But this time, I plan on being on top of the water and not underneath it," she explained.

"Right!" I nodded my head in agreement as I felt myself getting more excited. "Who were you planning to invite to the party?" I asked Julia absentmindedly as I was still thinking about diving.

"Well, let's see. You, obviously... and who else." Julia pressed her lips together as she thought about her group of friends. Using right hand, she ticked off a list of names. "I think I'll invite Michelle, Olivia, Emma, and Annisa."

Great, I thought. I smiled outwardly at Julia, but I groaned inwardly. Olivia, Emma, and Michelle were nice, and I got along with them even though I didn't know them well. I was bummed Julia was going to invite Annisa to the bachelorette party, but I shouldn't have been surprised she would be invited. If I was Julia's best friend, then Annisa would be Julia's second closest friend.

After Julia and I graduated from college eight years ago, I left Seattle to take my first teaching job overseas while Julia stayed to get her master's degree at Seattle University. Although we stayed in touch frequently, it wasn't the same, and Julia struck up a friendship with a girl who was also getting her master's degree in biomedical engineering at the university. While I lived overseas teaching English, Julia and Annisa forged their friendship over late-night studying sessions and writing their theses. What made it worse for me was that not only was Annisa smart, but she was gorgeous, which made me feel self-conscious around her.

Also, both Julia and Annisa were naturally slender and could eat whatever they wanted without gaining weight. I chafed whenever Annisa claimed she had to eat a candy bar every day to fit into her clothes. When Annisa made those comments around me, I wanted to toss whatever I was eating away.

And while Annisa seemed oblivious to the fact that other people had to watch their weight, Julia had more emotional intelligence and refrained from making comments that made people feel bad about themselves.

Julia's consideration of other people was her top quality, and it was what attracted me to Julia as a friend. So, having to spend a few days with Annisa was a small price to repay my friend's kindness throughout the years of our friendship. And if I volunteered to arrange the activities for the group, I might be able to find a way to indulge in my favorite pastime of scuba diving and avoid spending time with Annisa. That thought cheered me up.

"As your maid of honor, I would love to plan the trip," I said to Julia.

"That would be sweet of you. Thank you!" Julia smiled at

me. I grinned back and crossed my fingers Julia wouldn't detect how much Annisa bothered me. I also thought if I planned the outing, I could look at more affordable hotels. While the rest of the girls had jobs that paid more, I always seemed to be on a budget. Being a teacher was rewarding, but it didn't pay well. Despite the low salary, I loved being around my students.

Excited by the idea of seeing my best friend in a few months and going back to one of my favorite dive sites, I ended the Face-Time call by asking Julia to hug Grumpy and kiss him on the nose. At the mention of his name, the adorable Jack Russell Terrier approached the phone and came into view.

"How's my little Grumpy?" I cooed excitedly at the pup.

In response, Grumpy bumped his nose into the phone, so it took over the entire screen. Julia and I laughed at him, and she said, "Well, it appears Grumpy is looking forward to seeing you too!" I gave the little puppy a big smile and waved at my friend one last time before I pushed the end-call button. I sighed and shrugged my shoulders in contentment.

Then, I looked around the living room and thought of what I wanted to make for dinner. I rummaged through the kitchen and made myself some warm pita bread I bought earlier in the day at the market and served it with some hummus. As I sat eating my dinner out on the balcony, I admired the setting sun. The entire sky lit up in red, pink, and orange light as the sun sank below the horizon. The setting sun reminded me of another place with beautiful sunsets, and I sighed thinking about diving into the clear blue waters of the Caribbean Sea.

Chapter Two

"Please fasten your seatbelt and prepare for landing," the pilot announced.

I squirmed in my narrow economy seat anxious to get off the airplane. Even though the flight from San Francisco to Cozumel was less than six hours long, I had spent sixteen and a half hours on an airplane the week before coming back to San Francisco from Manama, Bahrain. The only good thing about the flight back to the United States was that the aircraft was almost empty because I flew on Christmas Day, which meant I had an entire row to myself. I took advantage of the perk and used all three seats to stretch out. However, this flight to Cozumel was packed with people trying to squeeze in one more vacation after the new year.

I gazed out the window of the aircraft as it made its final approach for landing. When the airplane lowered one of its wings as it circled the island, I saw the vibrant aqua-colored water off the coast.

As the plane touched down on the runway, I was thrust forward, and to steady myself, I braced my hands on the back of the seat in front of me. I must have pressed too hard because the person in front of me turned his head to peek through the gap.

"I'm so sorry," I mumbled. I cringed. My voice sounded like I had pebbles in my mouth because I had woken up a few moments ago.

The other girls and I from the bachelorette party picked a red-eye flight to Cozumel to save a couple of vacation days. This way we only had to take off a few days from work. Of course, taking time off was not an issue for me because I was currently out of a job, and I was waiting to hear back from the new schools I had applied to. I decided not to extend my teaching position in Manama because I wanted to live someplace new.

At my apology, the man in front of me nodded and said, "No problem." And he turned back to face the front. I couldn't tell if the guy was good-looking or not based on the small profile I saw, but he had a nice voice. My thoughts on the guy were disrupted when I heard a voice from a few rows behind me say loudly, "Ugh! I can't wait to get off this plane. My legs are asleep."

Without turning my head back to see who had made that remark, I identified the voice as Annisa Choi's. I sighed and rolled my eyes and silently prayed Annisa's diva ways wouldn't get to me during the trip.

"Breathe in, breathe out," I repeated softly to myself as the airplane descended.

The aircraft came to a complete stop about two hundred yards from the terminal building. I could see the runway workers push a giant staircase to the airplane door so we could disembark.

Since Julia and I were seated closest to the exit, we waited at the bottom of the stairs until the entire bachelorette party was off the plane.

"Wow, feel the warmth of the sun!" Emma said as she tilted her face upwards. The sunlight was so bright she reached into her purse and grabbed her sunglasses to put on her face. Emma Patel was from London, but she moved to the U.S. to get her graduate degree at Cal Berkeley and met Julia when they both worked at the same genetic startup, GENTEC. I had only met Emma a few times, but I loved her cheerful personality.

"This feels so much better than the wet and cold weather we left six hours ago in San Francisco," I agreed. The others nodded their heads as we followed the gaggle of tourists to the immigration line.

"How long do you think it will take us to get through this?" Julia asked me.

"I don't know," I replied.

"I hope we don't end up waiting forever!" Annisa whined looking around us as we snaked through the line towards the officials. Our fears were unfounded, and in less than twenty minutes we had our passports stamped.

"That was quick!" Emma said in surprise. "And look, our luggage is ready to be picked up.

Sure enough, the baggage handlers had moved all the suitcases off the conveyor belt to a corner where they were placed in neat rows. As I looked for my bags, I noted the numerous dive bags.

I looked through the random assortment of scuba brands before I spotted my neon pink dive bag. Not only was the bright color easy to spot, but I made sure I could easily identify which bag was mine by securing a hieroglyphic luggage tag with my name on it. I got the tag made as a souvenir on one of my dive trips to Egypt.

Other than the gear bag, I just had my carry-on suitcase, so I waited for the other ladies to find their bags which took a little longer since most of them had checked in dark-colored suitcases.

Without wasting any more time, we walked out of the baggage area to the transportation section where there were multiple kiosks manned by friendly and English-speaking guides waiting to help us.

"*¡Hola, amiga!* My name is Cassandra. Can I help you arrange transportation to your hotel?"

"*Sí, gracias.*" I replied in Spanish. Cassandra cocked her head to one side and said, "*¡Bueno! ¿Hablas español?*"

"*Sí, pero hablo Español un poco y no bien,*" I said.

"Okay, I'll speak in English then." Cassandra gave me a friendly nod that told me she appreciated the attempt at speaking the host country's language. One thing that I found out as I traveled internationally was that people were more hospitable and patient with foreigners if they tried to speak their language.

Cassandra launched into her planned spiel about all the different transportation options, and when I finished listening to the obligatory speech, I arranged for the bachelorette party to take a private shuttle to our resort hotel. As we made our way out of the airport, I noticed several groups were waiting in separate lines.

"Which line are we supposed to be in?" Olivia Lee asked as she surveyed the multiple queues. Olivia and Michelle Clark were Julia's friends from her internship days in Seattle. Like me, they still stayed in touch with Julia after she moved from Seattle to San Francisco.

Before I could reply to Olivia's question, I heard Annisa say, "Why don't you ask someone, Claire, since you've been here before?" I looked at Annisa who had put on an oversized floppy straw hat to match the large black sunglasses on her face. I smothered a laugh. Who does she think she is? A glamorous movie star?

"Sure," I said stifling any unpleasant comment I was thinking. I looked around to see if there was anyone that looked like they were part of the transportation company. Thankfully, there was a man a few feet away that was wearing a light blue polo shirt that said, "shuttle" with a picture of a van on the shirt.

"Disculpe, señor." I lightly tapped the man on the shoulder to get his attention. The man turned around and said, *"Sí, señorita.* Can I help you?"

I showed him the shuttle tickets I was holding in my hand. The van attendant looked at the tickets before he took them and walked over to a line of parked vehicles. I watched as the man spoke with a driver, and a few seconds later, he waved his hand for us to come to the van.

"Is this the van we need to get in?" I asked when we approached closer.

"Sí, señorita. The driver will take you to the resort you will be staying at. Also, if it is possible, would your group mind if three other people go with you because they are also staying at the same place?"

I shrugged and said, "Sure if there is room." The man smiled in thanks, and then he waved his hand to a group of guys standing by the curb. They immediately grabbed their bags and headed toward us.

When the guys reached where we were waiting, one of them said, "Thanks for letting us ride with you. We just missed the shuttle for our hotel, and we would have had to wait at least an hour for another ride. By the way, my name is Ryan."

Ryan had dark brown hair, which was cut short like a military haircut, but he didn't seem like he was in the military because he was wearing brightly colored Ray Ban Wayfarer sunglasses.

"No problem! I'm glad we have room." I replied to Ryan as I noticed he had a boyish look on closer inspection.

"I'm Aiden," said the other guy next to Ryan. He had a nice, deep voice. Aiden was taller than Ryan and had dark hair that was short but not as short as Ryan's.

"Hi, I'm Claire," I said to the guys. I was about to introduce the rest of the girls, but I was interrupted by the last guy.

"And I'm Andrew Markle, but you can call me Drew."

Drew looked older than Aiden and Ryan. He was sporting mirrored aviator sunglasses that hid the color of his eyes.

Even though he had gray hair around his temple, he looked fit as though he spent a lot of time at the gym. But what really stood out to me was a large red and white scuba diving flag tattooed on Drew's left bicep. The message he was trying to send wasn't very discreet, and I had to stop myself from giggling out loud.

"Ah-hem!" Annisa said clearing her throat. "Why don't we finish introducing ourselves in the van so we can get to the hotel?" She gave a coquettish smile at the van driver. He blushed in response and opened the passenger door for her.

As Annisa climbed into the van, Drew's eyes followed her backside.

"The way that dude is checking out Annisa is creepy," Emma whispered to me.

"I know!" I shuddered.

"Would you like to go in next?" Aiden gestured for me to go in the van.

"Thank you, but I was going to sit in the front." I gave Aiden a goofy grin unnerved by his good looks.

Unaware of the effect he had on me, he nodded and climbed in.

I let out the breath I was involuntarily holding. *This vacation is turning out to be interesting*, I thought as I opened the front passenger door.

Chapter Three

"¿Señor? How long does it take to get to our hotel?" I interrupted our van driver, Enrique, who was singing along to a song on the radio. He had a pretty good voice.

"Oh- about *diez minutos*."

We squealed in delight at Enrique's answer.

"Except, it's only ten o' clock in the morning, and we can't check into our rooms until three o'clock in the afternoon," Michelle said, looking down at her watch.

"That's a bummer," Olivia groaned.

"We can still store our luggage with the valet. Then, we can have an early lunch and drinks by the pool," Emma said, brightening everyone's morale.

"A frozen margarita sounds perfect right now," Julia said as we murmured in agreement.

"It does sound good, but I'm not going to drink because I signed up for an afternoon dive with the resort dive shop. I'm going to stick with drinking water, so I don't get dehydrated," I replied.

"Oh, you're a diver," Drew said from the back. He had been

quiet since we got into the van, but now he was interested in our conversation.

I swiveled my head around to respond to him, but before I could, he started to talk.

"I'm a diver too. In fact, I have over 300 dives," he volunteered.

I nodded politely, and I caught Aiden's gaze who was sitting in front of Drew. Seeing his eyes in the rearview mirror, it dawned on me that it was Aiden's eyes I saw between the crack of the airplane seats. I was going to comment I was the one who sat behind him on the airplane when Drew asked if anyone else dove.

The other women shook their heads, but Ryan spoke up.

"Aiden and I are here for our referral dives. We did the pool sessions and academics back in California, but we didn't want to do our check-out dives in the bay. It's too cold!"

"Just like Claire and I did many years ago," said Julia.

Drew looked at me and said, "Really? How many dives do you have?" The question itself was harmless, but for some reason, the way he brought it up made it sound like a challenge.

"So how many dives do you have?" Drew asked again impatiently. He looked at me expecting to hear a lower number of dives than his 300, but I looked squarely at him and answered, "I have 450 logged dives."

Ryan whistled, impressed.

Both Aiden and Ryan suppressed a smirk as they watched Drew's face become deflated when he realized I was more experienced than he was.

Not to be upstaged by me, Drew asked, "Yeah, but are you certified as a dive master?"

"No, I'm not."

"Too bad. I got my certification last year in Florida." Drew's eyes narrowed as he challenged me to top his credential.

I sighed. It was too early in the morning to be combative, so

I said, "That's great." I reached down to raise the volume knob on the radio discouraging any further talk with *mariachi* music.

I glanced at the rearview mirror at the other girls, and none of them were paying attention to the conversation. Even Aiden and Ryan were absorbed in their own discussion. How I got stuck talking to Drew was beyond me. I sighed again and turned to look out the window to the colorful shops along the street.

The last time I visited Cozumel, I came by myself. I stayed at one of the hostels in the downtown square. The area was busy day and night, and it was hard to wind down due to the noise. For the bachelorette weekend, I wanted to choose a location that was further removed from the tourist scene, and the rest of the girls even Annisa agreed.

Soon the shops thinned out as the shuttle van left the tourist center and headed along the coast toward the southern part of the island. It wasn't too long before the van slowed down to turn into a circular driveway.

"Okay, here we are. This is your hotel," Enrique said and turned off the engine.

A uniformed concierge opened the door and helped us out of the vehicle. Before I could ask if the others wanted to pool their money for the driver, Aiden said, "Since we crashed your private shuttle, I'd be happy to leave the tip."

"Thanks, Aiden." Julia beamed a smile at him.

"Yeah, thanks buddy," Drew said and clapped a hand on Aiden's shoulder. Then he quickly retrieved his bags and headed toward the front desk. The others followed Drew into the massive hotel.

When I got to the entrance, I looked up at the high ceiling and thought how much more impressive the resort was in-person than from the pictures online. I chose the place because the rooms were highly rated for its luxurious amenities, but most importantly, it had its own dive shop and pier located on the resort property.

"Wow, this place is incredible!" I heard a voice behind me say in awe. Aiden had tipped the driver and was now standing behind me taking in the elegant surroundings.

"Isn't the décor beautiful? It's both traditional and modern," I said.

Aiden nodded in agreement and said, "You mentioned you had an afternoon dive scheduled."

"That's right." I looked at him curiously.

"We're here early, so I'm going to find out if Ryan and I can join you." He gave me a shy smile.

"That would be great," I said excitedly. "The dive shop is down past the pool. Why don't you stow your luggage with the concierge and then check if there are any more openings for the 4:00pm dive?"

"Sounds like a good idea." Aiden's face lit up, and he gave me another smile before walking away.

Hmm... he seemed like a nice guy. My mind started to buzz, and I wanted to replay my conversation with him, but I realized I had no idea where my friends were. I looked around, but they weren't in the lobby.

They must be at the pool. I remembered Emma saying something about lunch and drinks.

"This is sweet," I said when I saw the large kidney-shaped pool with the swim-up bar. It was at the far end of the bar that I spotted my friends. They had staked out a table and had drinks already in their hands.

"Claire, over here!" Julia waved her hand over her head to catch my attention. I waved back and headed over to the table.

"Hi. I see you started without me."

"*Señorita*, would you like something to drink?" asked a waiter who appeared magically at the table.

"*Sí, Me gustaría beber agua por favor*," I replied in Spanish.

"*Bueno*," said the waiter and moved toward the bar to place my drink order.

"What time is your dive?" asked Julia, sipping on a frozen margarita. It looked refreshing, and for a split second, I regretted signing up for the trip.

"I'm scheduled for a sunset dive leaving the pier at 4:00pm."

"What's a sunset dive?" asked Olivia. She was holding something that had a tropical umbrella.

"It's pretty much the same as the other dives except the dive is timed so you surface just as the sun is setting. This way you have a pretty boat ride back to the resort," I explained.

"That sounds lovely!" said Emma in her British accent and took a sip of her tutti-frutti drink.

Yes, it would, I thought, especially if Aiden was able to get a spot on the dive. I just met him, but I was already attracted to his easy going and thoughtful manner.

My thoughts on Aiden were interrupted by Annisa. "It's difficult to choose," I heard her say.

As usual, she was holding court with the ladies. Being the center of attention was one of her annoying traits. I shook my head as she detailed her current dating life, which consisted of going out with several different guys she met through a dating app.

Maybe I was old-fashioned, but I didn't see how anyone could find dates through this way. I was also too self-conscious to post a picture that was flattering but at the same time not screaming, *the photo has been filtered and photoshopped!*

"Who do you like dating the most?" Michelle asked. She seemed genuinely interested in her answer.

"Well, it depends." Annisa drew out the word *depends,* making it more dramatic. "I think Hudson's the most attractive, but Micah has the best job. He's a sports agent for few of the players for the Bay Area Ballers."

"Really?" Impressed, Michelle's mouth opened slightly.

Annisa glowed as she basked in the limelight.

Puh-leeze, I thought and rolled my eyes. I couldn't take any more of Annisa's stories and made fidgeting movements with my head. When I got Julia's attention, I shot a look at Annisa.

I discreetly pointed towards the beach indicating I wanted to head out towards the dive shop. Julia nodded imperceptibly while keeping her attention focused on what Annisa was saying.

"Freedom," I whispered as I snuck my way toward the pier.

With my back turned, I didn't see Annisa smirk at me. Nor did I see her spot Aiden and Ryan heading towards the bar. Her face broke out in a huge smile as the two guys sat down at a table nearby.

Chapter Four

The dive shop was busy with activity. The boat from the second morning dive had arrived.

People were milling around and rinsing off their gear in a large basin filled with fresh water. I observed the scene and wondered how the dive went, and I soon got my answer.

"I'm so tired. The current was strong today." A dainty Asian woman wearing a full-length wetsuit told her husband.

The man made a grunting sound in agreement as he carried his gear to the rinse basin to wash off the salt from his equipment.

"Is everything okay?" the lady asked me. I didn't realize I had stopped walking and was standing in the middle of the wooden path over the sand. I must have zoned out because the woman was looking at me with a concerned expression. Her husband also stopped what he was doing to look at me.

"Oh, I'm fine," I stammered. I was embarrassed the woman caught me daydreaming. "I was just wondering how the dive trip went," I added, hoping my statement would make me seem more lucid.

"It was beautiful," the woman said. "The water was so clear

you could see out 100 meters. And I picked the wrong wetsuit to wear today. The water was very warm, and a shorty wetsuit would have been more comfortable."

"Also, the current was really strong, and it even switched directions while we were diving," the man added. "However, our guide was fantastic, and he kept us close to the wall and out of the current most of the time."

"Wow, I can't wait for my trip!" I said thinking about being in the water.

"When are you going? By the way, my name is Margaret Tanaka, and this is my husband, Tom."

"Hi, it's nice to meet you! I'm Claire O'Keefe."

Margaret's eyes widen in confusion when she heard me say my last name.

"I'm half Korean." They both nodded and said, "ahh!" Everything made sense to them now.

"I just arrived this morning, but I'm going on the sunset dive this afternoon," I added.

"Oh, that's great. We went on the sunset dive yesterday, and the setting sun was so exquisite," remarked Margaret. "We have plans to go on a Mayan ruin tour after we finish here; otherwise, we would have signed up to join you this afternoon. This is our first time to Cozumel, and we had no idea the diving would be this excellent. If we had known this, we wouldn't have bothered to make arrangements for other activities. But since we already paid for the excursions, we feel like we have to go. Both Margaret and Tom looked a little wistful thinking about the lost dives they could have had if they didn't go on the land tours.

"Oh!" I looked at my watch, and it read 2:45pm. I gave Margaret an apologetic look and said, "I need to go. It's a little early, but I hope the front desk will let me check in."

"Yes, yes, go ahead!" said Margaret shooing me away with her hands.

"I hope the current lessens up," Tom added. He was now rinsing off his wife's gear. I smiled at his thoughtfulness.

"I hope so too!" I replied as I waved goodbye to the Tanakas and headed to the concierge's desk to retrieve my bags.

They waved back and Margaret called out, "have a great time, and we'll see you tomorrow morning if you are diving again."

I gave them a thumbs up and quickly headed to the lobby.

Fortunately, the front desk clerk was very helpful and told me I could check in, but I needed Julia to sign the paperwork because she paid for the room.

When I was searching online for hotel deals, I wanted the bachelorette party to stay at a different resort, but Annisa, of course, didn't like my first choice saying it wasn't fancy enough, so after a few more options were looked at, we ended up choosing Cozumel Grand. However, the hotel was more expensive than I would have liked, and Julia, being the sweet and kind person she was, offered-no, more like-insisted she would pay for our room as a gift to me for agreeing to be her maid of honor.

"Shouldn't it be the other way around? Shouldn't I be the one to pay for the room since you're the one who is getting married?" I recalled telling Julia.

"True, but how many times did you come to San Francisco to see me in between your teaching jobs, and how many times have I visited you in the places that you lived?" inquired Julia.

"That's true...," Julia hadn't ever visited me overseas. Still, it didn't seem right my best friend was paying for the entire hotel lodging during her bachelorette party, but there was no way I would be able to convince Annisa to stay at any place less posh. So, I had to swallow my pride and accept Julia's offer.

With the afternoon dive starting shortly, I had no time to waste. I quickly walked to the pool area but stopped short of the bar because I didn't want to get sucked up in the conversation. I tried to get Julia's attention by waving both hands over my head.

This action worked, but it also got the attention of everyone else at the pool bar. The ladies looked at me and waved me over, but I stood firm. I pointed at my watch and gave an apologetic shrug. I pointed at Julia and motioned her to come over. My friend looked confused, but she finally got up from her chair and walked over.

"What's up? Why didn't you come over?" Julia asked.

"Yeah, I didn't want to get caught up in small talk because I want to get checked in, but the front desk needs you to sign the paper." I filled her in the details quickly.

"Ah, gotcha!" Julia nodded, and we walked with a purpose to the front desk clerk to sign the paperwork. It didn't take long to check-in as Julia had already paid for the room.

When the clerk handed Julia a small white envelope with the room number written on one side, she opened it to find two credit card sized key cards. She took one of them and handed it to me.

I promptly took the card and gave Julia a big bear hug. I knew I was acting like a maniac rushing my friend through the check-in process, but I hated to be late for anything, especially diving.

"Thank you so much!"

Julia laughed and said, "You're welcome! You better hurry and get changed, or the afternoon boat will leave without you.

I gave her another hug and grabbed my bags.

"You don't have to tell me twice!" I grinned at my best friend.

"Eek!" I squealed in delight as I rode the elevator to the room.

Chapter Five

The resort's diving outfit, Scuba Mar, was a big company, and it offered a twenty percent discount on all prepaid dives. For a budget-conscious person like me, the offer was very appealing.

The whiteboard hanging next to the office door showed that only one boat was going out in the afternoon. My pulse quickened when I saw that Aiden and Ryan were signed up for the trip.

"Ugh!" I groaned. Drew was also going on the dive. I sighed and hoped I would be able to limit my contact with him.

I headed out to the pier and went to stand by the boat which was aptly named "*Bonita*." It was a newly built and roomy.

As I was admiring the setup, I heard a voice inside the boat say, "*¡Hola, amiga!* Are you going on this trip?"

"Yes, I am."

"*Bueno!* My name is Marcos, and I'm going to be one of your guides today. Hand me your bags, and I will put them on a seat."

I passed him my mesh bag along with my pink waterproof

sack. After Marcos set them on a bench, he turned to me again and reached out a hand to help me in the boat.

"*Gracias,*" I said and looked around. The boat was already loaded with the air tanks. I counted six tanks, one for each diver. I wondered who else was coming.

Drew's loud and boastful voice drifted toward us. He was walking next to Ryan and Aiden, and he was talking to them about some trip he went on. Neither one of them seemed interested, and they walked faster, hoping to get away.

Drew didn't seem to notice their efforts to evade him, and he droned on about his adventures.

"*¡Hola, amigos!* A tanned young man who was in his mid to late twenties walked up behind the guys. He also had dark, curly hair that was kept on the longer side. However, what made him handsome was his bright and friendly smile.

"*¡Hola!*" I called back to him.

The young man caught up to the three Americans and gave them a smile. "*¡Hola!* Who is Ryan, and who is Aiden?"

"We are," said the guys at the same time. Then they realized their response wasn't helpful identifying who was who, so Aiden pointed a finger at himself, and said, "I'm Aiden, and he's Ryan" as he gestured toward his friend.

"*Bueno.* I have your rental gear here," the man said as he lifted the Buoyancy Control Devices (BCDS) and hoses. "I will set up everything for you, so you can get in the boat."

"Fantastic!" said Aiden excitedly as he quickly got in the boat with Ryan hopping in right after him.

"I'll put my own gear together," said Drew as he tried to call the attention back to him.

The young diving guide smiled and nodded, indicating that was okay, but he didn't engage Drew in further conversation.

Drew looked a little disappointed he wasn't given an opportunity to show off his knowledge.

For the next several minutes, we were busy setting up our

gear and fitting the hoses on the air tanks and checking the correct amount of gas-mixture for our trip.

"Okay guys, my name is Marcos, and that's Carlos over there," he explained as he pointed to the young guide who had finished setting up Aiden's and Ryan's scuba gear on the air tanks. Then he pointed to another man, who looked much older than Marcos and Carlos, and said, "this is Pablo, your boat captain."

"We're going to take you this afternoon to dive *Chankanaab*. It will take about ten to fifteen minutes on the boat. We are very lucky right now because the winds are calm, so the water is like glass, and the current is mild. Earlier today, the current was stronger." This reminded me of the conversation I had with the Tanakas, and I was glad the situation had changed in the water.

"There are only four divers today because two people canceled, so each diving pair will have their own personal guide," Marcos added with a laugh. I was glad the groups were small because I had been on dives where it was common for each dive guide to go with six to eight divers in the group.

"Since Aiden and Ryan are going to be doing two of their four check-out dives, they will be going with me, and we are going to do the skills in the lagoon where there is no current. Carlos will take Claire and Drew on their dive drifting south with the current. By the time Claire and Drew are ready to surface, Aiden and Ryan should be done with their skills, and then we can pick up Claire and Drew."

The dive plan Marcos had outlined made a lot of sense, and even if I had to partner with Drew, I was determined to enjoy my time in the water as much as I could.

"Does anyone have any questions?" asked Marcos looking around the boat. Seeing the divers shake their heads, he turned to Pablo, and said, "Okay Pablo. *¡Vamos!*

The boat captain gave a small salute and started the engine.

Pablo expertly reversed the boat away from the pier and headed out to sea.

As the boat picked up speed, I sat back against the plastic bench and looked at the beautiful turquoise water. I could hardly believe how lucky I was to be back in Cozumel scuba diving.

The waves crashed against the boat, and I could feel how warm the water was as the droplets hit my arm. I recalled the first time Julia and I came to Cozumel to do our check-out dives for our open water certification. That was ten years ago when Julia and I were sophomores in college.

I met Julia during my first year at Seattle University when we were both in the freshman chemistry class. It turned out we were both science majors. However, by the time our sophomore year rolled around, I was burned out with the sciences and turned to major in English. I remembered how devastated my mother was when I told her I was switching majors. Like most Asian parents, Mona, valued academics above all things, especially academic fields that held prestige and earned a higher income. My mom's admonishment was still etched in my memory even though that was ten years ago.

"What! Why do you want to study English? You already know English! Why don't you study engineering? Engineers make a lot of money," Mona clucked her tongue in disapproval.

Thankfully, my American-born dad, Tim, was more sympathetic and understood there was value in other degrees and encouraged me to switch majors.

"It's fine, Claire," my dad said when I told him I wouldn't make as much money being an English teacher compared to being an engineer. "Money isn't the only thing that is important in life," he added.

"But money, is very helpful," shot back Mona as she overheard her husband's conversation with her daughter.

I rolled my eyes and shrugged my shoulders. My dad was

more encouraging about my future than my mom was because he also had an undergraduate degree in English. After graduation, he took a job teaching English at a university in Seoul, South Korea where he met my mom. My mom liked to tell me if she hadn't married my father, she would have become a successful doctor in Korea.

Before my mother championed the idea of me becoming an engineer, she pushed the idea of me being a doctor. Unfortunately, I was uncomfortable around people in pain and could not stand the sight of blood, so to my mother's chagrin, being a doctor was out of the picture.

Now my old college roommate was on her way to becoming a respected stem cell researcher in the Bay Area while I was traveling around the world teaching English.

Sitting on the boat with the afternoon sun on my face, and the wind blowing through my hair, I felt grateful for the experiences I had. I just wished I had more friends that scuba dove.

Other than Julia, no one else in the bachelorette group had a scuba diving certification.

The sound of the boat's diesel engine brought me back from daydreaming, but the loud chugging noise made it impossible to have a conversation with anyone on the boat unless I wanted to shout.

While everyone was trying to enjoy the afternoon, Drew started droning on about the other places he dove.

I rolled my eyes at his stories that were most likely embellished, but he was too caught up in his own narration to see my facial expression. However, Carlos saw me make a face, and he smiled and winked at me. I smiled back enjoying our shared secret.

As Drew carried on about his diving adventures, he dispensed unsolicited advice about the best way to conserve air or achieve neutral buoyancy.

"The best way to achieve neutral buoyancy is ..." Fortunately, I did not have to continue listening to Drew over the boat's engine as Marcos shouted that we were a few minutes away from the dive site.

"Yes!" I exclaimed gleefully.

Aiden and Ryan laughed at my enthusiasm.

I caught Aiden looking at me, and I quickly turned away in embarrassment. I didn't know what was wrong with me. Why was I feeling so flustered? I needed to snap out of it before he thinks I'm some sort of weirdo.

Chapter Six

"I'm going diving, I'm going diving." I repeated the mantra in my head. It was hard to stay optimistic when the guy that was supposed to keep me safe kept cracking stupid jokes.

"Wow, that's all the air that you have in the tank?" He remarked in mock surprise when he turned the air handle.

"What?" I grabbed my air gauge and looked down at the reading. "What do you mean that's all the air that I have. The gauge is reading 3000 psi, and that should be enough for this dive."

"Just kidding," Drew laughed. "I wanted to see your reaction when I said you didn't have enough air."

I gave a feeble chuckle in response, but I silently fumed in my head. Who joked about air when you were about to go underwater. It was like joking about having a bomb in your carry-on case right as you were about to board a plane. Only an obtuse person like Drew would think it would be funny. I gritted my teeth.

By the time we reached the lagoon, we managed to finish the pre-dive check without further incident.

"I'm going to jump in first. Then Aiden and Ryan will go next," Marcos said before he took a giant stride into the water.

Carlos waited until Ryan popped out of the water before he went in. When he surfaced out of the water, he said, "okay, now your turn Claire."

Placing the regulator in my mouth, and with one hand on my mask, so it wouldn't slip off, I took a giant stride off the ledge of the boat and felt the rush of water as I impacted the sea.

Once I surfaced, I made the okay signal and waited for Drew to jump in next. When all three of us were ready to go under, Carlos put his thumb down which was the sign to descend. I exhaled out of my regulator and felt myself start to sink towards the bottom with the help of the weights that I had in my BCD.

The immediate feeling of calm set upon me as I descended. By the time I reached the top of the reef, I was determined to have a great dive despite having an irritating partner.

The *Chankanaab* reef teamed with marine life, and I enjoyed taking video of all the colorful fish. I was in a great mood when we surfaced the water and waited for Pablo and his boat to find us. It didn't take the boat captain long to find us. We were floating near a bright orange surface marker. He raised his hand in greeting as he turned off his engine to let the boat drift closer.

Even though Carlos was the closest one to the boat, he motioned for Drew or me to go first.

"Hey, what are you doing?" I said in surprise as I felt Drew push me aside.

"I'm trying to get to the ladder." He gave a look that said *isn't it obvious*?

I wasn't going to argue and let him swim past me.

I waited until Drew and his dive gear were in the boat before I swam for the ladder. Carlos was floating next to it and said to me, "Claire, why don't you give me your fins so I can hand them to Pablo, and then you can climb up the ladder." I smiled and wished more guys were like him.

I climbed up the ladder and lifted my leg on the ledge, but it was difficult with the heavy BCD and air tank strapped on my back. I would have stumbled a bit, but Pablo was there to give me a hand and helped me to the bench. He pushed the tank back in its holding.

Once everyone was free from the scuba gear, we started to talk about the dives.

"It was incredible. I wasn't even nervous about taking my mask off and putting it back on underwater. I worried about doing this in open water because I had trouble with this skill in the pool." Ryan's animated face showed how elated he was. He added, "Marcos was such a great and patient instructor that I was able to do this skill correctly the first time."

Marcos smiled at the praise, and he lifted his right hand to give Ryan a high five, and said, "No problem *amigo*. You did awesome. A real natural!"

I clapped and gave Ryan an encouraging nod, and everyone was feeling happy for the two new divers, until Drew said, "You had trouble with that skill? Man, that was so easy!"

I glared at him. *What was wrong with this guy?*

Ryan pressed his lips together to prevent a retort from escaping. I didn't blame him. I didn't know if there was an appropriate answer to such a rude comment.

However, Marcos, having numerous years of customer service experience dealing with divers with all sorts of different personalities, smoothly said, "the mask flooding and taking it off and putting it back on is by far the most challenging skill for many people, and it was great Ryan and Aiden were able to do it correctly the first time." Then he quickly changed subjects so Drew wouldn't have time to add his opinion by pointing out the beautiful setting sun.

"Look at the horizon amigos. *Que bonita!*"

Even Drew was mesmerized by the pinks and purples in the sky as we watched the sun set as we motored back to the resort.

Just as the last ray of light faded to darkness, Pablo's boat pulled up to the pier. Carlos threw the nylon rope to one of the dive attendants so the boat could drift right next to the dock. Once the captain turned off the engine, we grabbed our gear bags and climbed out of the boat.

Since Aiden and Ryan were renting their gear, they didn't have to rinse out their equipment, but they walked with me towards the wash basin.

"What are you doing this evening?" asked Aiden. Having him so close to me made me feel a light-headed.

"I'm meeting the girls I'm here with for a bachelorette party for dinner," I replied as I dunked my BCD into the fresh water.

Aiden's lips dipped slightly in disappointment, but he recovered.

"That sounds like fun! I hope you have a great time."

"Bachelorette party, huh?" Drew said, looking interested.

"Are you going diving again tomorrow?" asked Aiden as he ignored Drew's comment.

"Yes, I booked two more days of two-tank dives".

"Cool! We have our last day of checkout dives tomorrow, but after that, we're planning to do another day of recreational diving," Aiden explained.

"Yeah, we want to get as many dives in as we can," added Ryan.

I really enjoyed Aiden and Ryan's company, and I wanted to keep talking to them, but I also wanted to get away from Drew, who kept lurking around. So, I quickly put my gear into the mesh bag.

"I'm glad you guys were able to go on the sunset dive and do your first two check-out dives. I'll see you tomorrow." I waved goodbye to the guys.

Drew had walked to the dive shop and was talking to Carlos, so I was able to make my getaway without being pestered. But I didn't want to be rude to Carlos, so I called out to them, "Have a good night! See you tomorrow."

Carlos smiled and waved goodbye, but Drew just stared after me.

Oh, thank goodness. I sighed as I walked past the pool that was illuminated with colored lights in the water. The tiki torches were spread throughout the beach and pool area were also lit making the ambiance more intimate. There were some people still swimming, but the area looked sparse compared to the afternoon.

A little boy splashed in the shallow end of the pool, and his mother desperately tried to get him out.

"Tommy let's go. It's time for dinner," the woman cried out in vain. He ignored her and went under the water. When the woman and I made eye-contact, she rolled her eyes.

"He always does this when it's time to eat. At this rate, we'll be eating dinner when it's past his bedtime."

I gave her a sympathetic smile and said, "Good luck. I hope you can get him out soon." I waved and continued to my room.

By now I was starving, and I was looking forward to meeting up with the rest of the ladies for dinner.

"Ugh!" I said under my breath. I remembered Annisa would be there. *Life would be so much easier if Julia and Annisa weren't good friends,* I thought as I pushed the elevator button.

Chapter Seven

I inserted my key card into the lock, and when the light turned green, I turned the handle and opened the door. The water was streaming in the bathroom. Julia was taking a shower, so I took out my wet gear from the mesh bag and laid it flat on the tile floor by my bed. I was careful not to fall on the cold, slippery surface as I placed my fins that were still wet on the floor.

It would be just my luck that I would injure myself during this vacation. And knowing Annisa would make some sort of remark regarding my clumsiness, I was extra careful where I placed my feet. After I was satisfied my gear was laid out properly to dry, I flopped on the double bed I staked out when I checked in and closed my eyes for a few minutes. Or at least that's what I intended to do, but I felt someone shake me awake.

"Huh, what's going on?" I mumbled and blinked a few times.

"You fell asleep," Julia explained as she stood over me fully dressed. She was wearing a blue strapless maxi dress that made her look shabby chic.

"Oh no, I only meant to close my eyes for a few minutes.

36

What time is it? Are we late?" I craned my head to look for the clock next to the bed stand, but I was too disoriented from my nap to make out the red, glowing numbers.

"It's 7:40pm," said Julia as she noted the time from her wristwatch. "We still have time before we have to meet the girls in the lobby. Why don't you take a quick shower and get dressed and meet us downstairs when you're done."

I sat up on the bed and said, "I'll be quick- you know me. I don't need a lot of time to get ready."

Julia nodded in agreement, and she waved goodbye as she left me to get ready for dinner. "Meet you downstairs in fifteen," she added before she opened the door.

"Okay!" I sprang into action and headed towards the bathroom.

When I arrived downstairs wearing some khaki cotton shorts and a white t-shirt, the girls were sitting down on the wicker furniture that was spread throughout the lobby.

Looking at their cute and colorful sundresses, I grimaced. I was the only one wearing shorts and a shirt. *Whoops, I guess I didn't get the memo.*

Michelle and Olivia already had drinks in their hands. They must have gotten down here early. I waved hi to them but didn't go over to them as I was looking for Julia. I scanned the lobby and spotted my friend standing next to Annisa and Emma. I started to walk towards them when I stopped in my tracks. To my dismay, Drew from the dive tour was talking to my friends.

"Ugh! Why can't I get rid of that guy!" I said quietly under my breath.

I debated whether I should keep my distance from the group, but Annisa saw me and waved me over. *Great!*

"Hey Claire! That's our friend who is also a scuba diver," she said to Drew. He turned to where Annisa was pointing at and said, "Fancy meeting you again!" He laughed as though he thought his comment was the funniest thing anyone had ever heard. I gave a slight smile and half-hearted wave.

Drew was wearing a bright yellow Hawaiian shirt that flattered his tanned skin. He would have been attractive if he wasn't so arrogant.

I didn't want to go over to my friends because of Drew, but there was no way I could do that without appearing anti-social which was something some people including two ex-boyfriends have accused me of being. For me, it wasn't that I was anti-social, but I was an introvert. It took tremendous energy talking to people, especially people I didn't know well or didn't like. I found it difficult to maintain romantic relationships because the guys I had previously dated liked to go out to social events whereas I enjoyed more low-key dating venues.

Plus, none of the guys I had dated were going to be long-term prospects because they didn't dive. I was at the point where I stopped trying to find someone to date because I found it awkward and exhausting trying to explain my social preferences.

Even though I had given up, Julia had not. She was more optimistic about my dating life, and she kept trying to set me up with her fiancé's friends. Right before we went to Cozumel, Julia had arranged a double date with her, her fiancé- Tristan Park, and Tristan's best man, Adam Bloomberg.

Julia thought Adam and I would get along well because we both liked to travel. Adam was a high school math teacher in San Francisco, and he was in the Navy Reserves. During the summer, he fulfilled his active-duty time serving in duty stations overseas. Once he fulfilled his work commitment, he took the rest of the summer to travel. At Julia's urging, I met Adam for coffee. I thought Adam was great, but he didn't scuba dive which was a non-starter in my book.

When I told Julia I didn't think Adam was someone who I could see myself with for the long haul because he wasn't a scuba diver, she pressed her lips together to keep her from berating me.

Instead, Julia told me I was too picky. Then she asked me why it was so important the guys I dated had to be scuba divers.

I explained to Julia dating a diver would make it easier to plan vacations because we would both want to go someplace to dive. And though Julia was disappointed I ruled out Adam as a potential boyfriend, the practical side of her saw the logic behind my answer. However, that didn't mean Julia had given up on my dating life as she vowed to continue to search for potential dates.

One person Julia knew that wasn't going to make my dating list even though he was a diver was Drew. She could see I was dragging my feet and wished Annisa had not called his attention to me, so she interrupted Annisa's monologue.

"Wow, look at the time. We better head down to the restaurant since we have reservations for 8:00pm." I looked down at my phone to confirm the time.

"Yeah, it's about that time. Let's go!" Emma said.

"Hey, can I join you all?" asked Drew. "It seems like we're enjoying each other's company."

I couldn't believe it! That was the cheesiest line I ever heard, and I couldn't believe the guy's audacity trying to crash a bachelorette dinner. I was wondering who would reply when Emma chimed in and said, "Sorry, mate! Ladies only."

Thank you, Emma! If it wouldn't be so out of place, I would have given Emma a hug in gratitude for saving me and the other ladies from prolonging the conversation with an egotistical man like Drew, but Emma had no idea of the favor she had done or what I was thinking. The only person that seemed disappointed was Annisa, who seemed to like the attention that Drew was bestowing on her.

She gave him a flirtatious smile, and he wiggled his eyebrows at her. I tried not to blanch as I witnessed their exchange.

"Okay, maybe I'll see you guys afterwards and have drinks," Drew said pointedly at Annisa. I avoided eye contact with him until we got out of the lobby and were on a wooden path that led to a separate building in the resort.

"I love the layout of the resort compound." I commented to Julia. I tried to erase the image of Drew and Annisa flirting with the beautiful landscape.

"Me too. I love how instead of one large concrete structure, there are several buildings, so they all have a different feel," Julia remarked.

It was true. I noticed when we first checked in, the main building consisted of the lobby, gift shop, bar, and hotel rooms, but there were three separate buildings for each of the resort's all-inclusive restaurants in addition to a building for the gym and a spa. There was even an adult only pool with its own bar that was separate from the main pool and bar. And of course, the dive shop was located near the pier for people who wanted to dive or do other water sports.

"I'm so stuffed. The food was delicious," Julia said and patted her stomach. She leaned back against the chair. "What do you guys want to do now?"

"I want to head back to the pool because the hotel staff was setting up a dance area." Olivia smiled in hopefulness.

"I'm okay with that," Julia looked at the rest of us. Michelle and Emma nodded in agreement, but Annisa said, "I'll go, but only if there are cute guys there. If we only see couples, I think we should take a cab downtown."

"You girls can go dancing without me. I'm going to bed." I let a big yawn.

"Are you tired from your dive?" Julia asked, and she patted my shoulder.

"Yes, and I'm going diving again in the morning," I said, feeling bad about ditching the girls. Although it was true that I was diving again, the real reason why I didn't want to go was because I was a bad dancer. While everyone did the latest dance move, I tried not to look like an idiot. The safest thing for me to do was to jump up and down with the beat. At least, I could keep a beat. I involuntarily shuddered when I pictured myself dancing.

The girls waved goodbye and headed out to the pool bar again. This time, there were more people as the dinner hour was over. In addition to more people, the music started playing loudly over the speakers. When I heard the house music, I sighed in relief that I wasn't out there trying to make conversation with people I could barely hear over the thumping music.

I opened the door to my room, but to my alarm, I could still hear the music. I walked over to the balcony that had a view of the sea and the pool area where I could see people now dancing with fluorescent lights by the pool.

"Well, I'm glad to see everyone's having fun!" I was genuinely happy for my friends enjoying themselves, but I wasn't a person that was comfortable in large gatherings. I knew Julia was more like me, but the other girls were social, and she wanted to make sure everyone was having fun.

The thought of diving tomorrow was my idea of fun, so I got into bed and turned off the lights. I still couldn't sleep with the music in the background, so I grabbed my phone next to the nightstand and scrolled through the screen until I found the app I wanted. I found the playlist for intense rain sounds that had a running time of ten hours. I hit play and when the sound of rain filled the room, I sighed in contentment.

Ah, much better! I drifted off to sleep thinking about the possibility of seeing a shark on the next day's dive.

Chapter Eight

I arrived at the dive shop with my gear just as it opened for business. Since they were not ready to load the passengers, I headed over to the bar to see if they had coffee. To my luck, the bar was open, and I was able to order a *café con leche*.

I sat on the barstool and enjoyed the tranquility around me. I was not an early riser but going scuba diving made it easier to get up with the rising sun.

While I was drinking my hot coffee, I saw a few other guests filtering in for the day's dive. It looked like the Tanakas and a younger woman who looked like she may be a solo diver. I glanced at the other woman with interest. Maybe, if I got along with her, I would ask if we could partner up. This way I could avoid being Drew's partner.

I set my empty coffee cup on the bar, and I walked over to the Tanakas.

"Good morning!" I called out in greeting when they saw me coming their way.

"Good morning, Claire," said Margaret, and her husband waved hello in greeting. "Did you have a nice sunset dive?"

"Yes, it was beautiful just as you said. We went to

Chankanaab. The reef was full of sea life, and on our trip back to the pier, the sunset was spectacular.

"That's great!" Margaret smiled widely at the description of the dive. "I wonder where we are going today?" Margaret asked as she looked for her husband who after waving hello to me meandered over to the dive shop. I was about to suggest we go over to the dive shop to look at the whiteboard by the door when Tom Tanaka stepped out of the dive shop lobby and headed our way.

"I talked to Marcos this morning, and we are going to the Palancar dive sites today." Tom looked extremely happy about the dive site locations.

"I love the Palancars!" I jumped up and down in excitement.

"And it looks like we have a large group today. There will be several boats for all the divers," Tom added.

"Gosh, I hope I'm able to get on a boat with people I know," I said as my excitement turned to worry. In addition to being partnerless, I hoped I didn't get assigned to a boat that had a large tour group where everyone else knew each other.

My fears were unfounded as Tom continued, "don't worry Claire. I saw on the whiteboard that you are on the same boat as us, Peyton, and some guys named Drew, Aiden, and Ryan. I knew who the guys were, but I didn't know who Peyton was.

"Have you met Peyton?" I asked the Tanakas.

"Oh yes," answered Margaret as she pointed to the woman that came with the couple. "She's really sweet. She's here with her parents, and they're staying at the resort too. We dove with her yesterday."

I was relieved to hear good things about Peyton, and I hoped I could buddy with Peyton rather than Drew today. Speaking of the devil, I heard the man in question before he arrived at the pier. I did an about-face to see Drew approaching the dive shop.

"This reminds me a lot of the time I was diving in the Maldives," I heard him say. But to who he was talking to was a mystery because I didn't see anyone paying attention him. It looked like everyone was either loading tanks or gear on the boat.

"Hey there, you!" Drew spotted me looking in his direction.

Oh no! I panicked and glanced around the area, but there was nowhere to escape without looking obvious, and the Tanakas had wandered off, so I couldn't pretend to talk to them. I stood rooted to the wooden planks of the pier watching Drew approach me eager to continue bragging about his diving exploits. He was only a few steps away from me when I heard a female voice say my name.

"Hi, are you Claire?" I turned to see the young woman that had been talking to the Tanakas. She was my height, but she had long, curly brown hair that was pulled into a low ponytail. She also had big, brown eyes making her look innocent.

"Yes, I am." I replied and smiled at her.

"Are you Peyton?"

The young lady smiled back in affirmation. "Marcos told me I should buddy with you this morning on our dives since both of us are solo divers."

"If Claire's going to dive with you, then who's going to be my partner?" While I was talking to Peyton, Drew had come up to us.

"I'm not sure. Maybe you should ask Marcos. He's the lead dive master," answered Peyton.

"I know who he is," answered Drew condescendingly.

"Good, then you shouldn't have any problems finding him," Peyton snapped back.

Ooh! I like her. Even though Drew was older, she didn't take any crap from him, and she wasn't afraid to speak up. My first impression of her was wrong. I think she and I will get along great! My day was starting to brighten up.

"Is it my imagination or is that guy kind of a jerk?" asked Peyton after Drew had walked off in a huff. He was probably going to complain to Marcos about having a good dive buddy.

"No... you're not imagining things, the guy is a world-class jerk," I answered. "I dove with him yesterday, and I was hoping I would be on a different boat than him, but at least I don't have to buddy with him today." I smiled at Peyton.

"Hi Claire!" Both Peyton and I turned to see who had called my name. It was Aiden, and he was walking with Ryan with their snorkeling gear.

"Hi Aiden. Hi Ryan. This is Peyton," I introduced the group. "We are all on the same boat along with Margaret and Tom Tanaka, and we also have Drew with us."

The guys' faces fell when they heard Drew was going to be on the boat with them, but they didn't have much time to show their displeasure because Marcos came out of the dive shop.

"*Buenos días amigos.* Are you ready to dive today?"

"*Sí*" I said as I heard the same answer echoed around the group that was scattered around the pier.

"We have a large group today, so let's start getting on the boats. If you don't know what boat you are on, you can come talk to me," Marcos said as everyone started to move with their gear.

Within minutes, the experienced crew had everyone loaded on the boat and all three dive boats were ready to head out to sea.

This morning, the group was heading towards the Palancar dive sites off the southwest coast of Cozumel. The Palancar coral reef was divided into several sections according to depth and formation features in the Marine National Park. Today, the dive boat was going to my favorite area which was the Palancar gardens. No matter how many times I dove through the arches of the Palancar gardens, I always saw something new.

From the corner of my eye, I saw Drew talking with Peyton. Judging from her expression she didn't seem too thrilled. I heard her say, "I'll think about it," and walk away.

Drew looked flabbergasted. He probably wasn't used to having people, especially women, walk away from him.

"What's so funny?" Aiden said when he saw me chuckling.

"Oh, it's nothing." I didn't want to say aloud what I was laughing about.

Aiden leaned towards me and said conspiratorially, "do you think Drew just got stood up by Peyton?"

I open my mouth in shock. I burst out laughing because Aiden had also witnessed Drew's attempt to pick up Peyton.

Aiden joined in. I found it endearing when his eyes crinkled as he laughed.

"I guess, we'll have to ask."

"What are you two snickering about?" Aiden and I didn't see Drew come up.

"We were wondering if we would see a shark on the dive," Aiden said with a dead pan expression.

"And that's funny? You guys are weird!" Drew gave a look of disgust and climbed in the boat.

We both chuckled again. Then Aiden climbed in the boat. Once he was in, he reached out his hand to help me in.

When my fingers touched his, I felt a tingling sensation. I held onto his hand a few seconds longer than needed to get into the boat before I reluctantly let go. "Thank you," I murmured.

"You're welcome," he said softly. My heart started to beat faster as I looked at his handsome face.

"Sweet- Caroline!" I heard a voice sing.

"Wha-?" I saw Drew at the center of the boat singing with his arm draped around Marcos. They were swaying to music.

Someone had hooked up their phone to a speaker.

I looked back at Aiden, but the moment was lost. However, he smiled at me.

I shrugged my shoulders to say *we might as well join in*, and I started to sing along with Drew and Marcos. By now, Drew was waving his arms like a conductor going from one person to the next. As the dive boat motored out to sea, the rest of us sang to Neil Diamond.

Chapter Nine

"Five minutes until we get to our dive site. Get ready everyone. It's time to have some fun!" Marcos shouted over the noise of the boat engine.

With anticipation, I started to pull up my 3mm neoprene wetsuit over my hips. "Ugh!" With a forceful tug, I finally managed to get on my wetsuit. Now I just had to get my fins and mask on and walk over to the end of the boat. From there, I would do a giant stride entry into the warm waters.

The boat stopped with the engine at an idle and the crew gathered to help each of the divers do a last-minute check to make sure their air was turned on. I was waiting patiently in line when I felt a push from behind.

"Hey-!" I cried, trying not to fall. I turned around to see Drew.

"Chill out, Claire bear! It was an accident," he said and smiled as if it was a great joke.

I clenched my jaws and took a deep breath through my nose. Drew came up with the annoying nickname *Claire bear* after the stuffed animal that was popular in the 80s on yesterday's dive. I wasn't sure if he was trying to be cute or make a snide comment about the extra pounds that I carried around my small frame.

I ignored Drew and tried not to let his rude behavior ruin my dive.

"¡Hola Claire!" said Carlos. "Are you ready?" I didn't see Carlos as he came from the front of the boat to check on the divers.

"¡Sí!" I replied.

"Bueno, vamos," he said and patted my back as he left to help the other divers go into the water.

On yesterday's sunset dive, the crew found out I spoke some Spanish and wanted to practice my language skills, so they started speaking Spanish with me while they spoke in English to everyone else. I was flattered, and everyone else didn't mind except for Drew who thought the crew was talking about him behind his back. It was mostly true.

Although they refrained from making really nasty remarks, which Drew deserved, they did call him nicknames and compared him to unflattering sea creatures. The best comparison I heard was when Pablo called him an octopus because he seemed to have thoughts on everything from the best type of underwater cameras to the best way to get rid of sea sickness. Every time Drew opened his mouth to talk, the crew just shook their heads in amusement.

Once the entire group was in the water, Marcos signaled to everyone to deflate our BCDs and descend. Prior to going into the water, Marcos briefed to us that we would descend to 80 feet and swim through the reef until we were low on air. When we reached about 700psi, we needed to start our ascent to do our safety stop at 15 feet for about three minutes.

When the last diver descended to about 80 feet, Marcos made another okay signal and waited for us to make an okay signal back to him before he leveled off and kicked his fins toward the opening of one of the numerous arches in Palancar Gardens.

As I kicked my fins behind me, I marveled at how warm and clear the water was. Even though the best visibility in the waters of Cozumel normally occurred during the summer months, I could easily see 30 to 40 feet ahead of me.

In addition to the amazing clarity of the waters, I was mesmerized by the variety of fishes that swam around me. It was like swimming in a tropical aquarium. After about ten minutes of drifting through the coral arches, I spotted a hawksbill turtle swimming underneath a coral ledge. I swam closer to the turtle to get a picture of the marvelous creature. Even though I had seen turtles in Cozumel before, I became excited every single time I saw one in person. The pictures I took of them didn't do these gentle creatures justice when I showed the digital photos to my land loving friends.

Off to the distance, I could see the groups of divers from other dive shops swimming with their dive master. Cozumel was a very popular dive site, and there were numerous dive operators on the island. When you were on top of the water, you could see the small dive boats that were chartered to take divers each day circling around looking for their divers. But under water, each dive master tried to separate themselves from the other groups. So even though our group was diving in the Palancar Gardens with several dozen divers, it seemed as though our group was only one in the sea, and that was how I liked it.

Chapter Ten

I checked my air gauge that was clipped to my BCD, and it read close to the 700 psi level. I swam towards Marcos and signaled to him I was getting low on air. He made an okay sign to acknowledge he understood me, and then he made a sign to ask everyone how they were doing on air.

It turned out everyone was getting close to the 700 psi threshold, so Marcos determined we should start our ascent together. All the divers made an okay sign with their hand, except for Drew who vigorously shook his head and pointed at his air gauge. He indicated with his fingers he had 1000 psi left in his air tank. Since no one else had that much air left, Marcos shook his head and signaled to start ascending.

Fortunately, the water muffled the sound that came from Drew's mouth, but I could only imagine the expletives that would be spewing out of his mouth if he hadn't had a regulator blocking the sounds.

Around fifteen feet from the surface of the water, the group made a safety stop. We needed to stay underwater for at least three minutes to let the nitrogen that had been building up in our bloodstream be released. With everyone else floating neutrally in the water, Drew swam over to me and wagged his finger. Even though his mask shielded a part of his face, I could clearly see the anger in his eyes. There wasn't much I could do, so I just shrugged my shoulders and avoided eye contact. Instead, I looked down at my dive computer.

According to my watch, I had about 30 more seconds in my safety stop. With Drew hovering beside me, I watched the seconds count down. Finally, my watch beeped indicating I could continue the ascent, and with relief, I slowly kicked my fins to propel me to the surface.

As soon as Drew broke the surface, he spit out his regulator.

"You know, if you tried to breathe more slowly, you could have done a better job conserving your air," Drew yelled out to me.

Aiden broke the surface close to us, so he heard Drew's insult. He pivoted in the water and said, "It's not Claire's fault we had to ascend. I was at 750 psi."

I looked at Aiden and smiled in thanks. Before Drew could make any more disparaging comments, the dive boat we came on arrived.

Today we were on a different boat with a new captain. The boat was named *Catalina* after the boat owner's, Raul, mother. During the ride out to the dive site, I asked Raul how he came to name the boat. He explained his mother loaned him the money many years ago to buy the *Catalina* that allowed him to be a dive boat captain. To honor his mother and her gift to him, Raul named his most prized possession after her. As the *Catalina* idled her engine, the crew lowered the ladder.

Once the engine was turned off, Marcos signaled to me I should swim to the ladder first since I was the closest to the boat. Anxious to get away from Drew and with just a few stokes of my arms, I was able to reach the aluminum ladder. I took off my BCD, and handed it to Miguel, one of the deck hands. Then, with one hand grabbing onto the ladder, I used the other hand to remove my fins and held them up for Miguel to take to my spot. Wearing the aluminum tank on my back, I walked unsteadily to my seat. At one point, I lost my balance and tipped back. If it weren't for Carlos, I would have fallen flat on my butt.

"*Cuidado* Claire!" said Carlos, but he was smiling, so I knew it was just a friendly warning.

"*Gracias* Carlos." I said and continued to walk to the front of the boat. By the time I arrived at the bench, I saw Miguel had changed out my air tank, but I checked to make sure that all the straps were on tight, and I looked at the air gauge to see how much air I had. The gauge read 3000 psi, and just to make sure I had air, I turned on the valve and pressed the button on my regulator to hear the hissing sound of the air that was being released out of the mouthpiece. Satisfied everything was in order for my next dive, I reached in my waterproof bag for my fleece jacket and water bottle.

Instead of providing packaged food during the surface interval, the crew provided fresh fruit they had cut up while we were in the water. Not only was the fruit a delicious snack, but it was also environmentally friendly because after the crew cut up the fruit, they put the fruit peels in a container that would be transferred to a compost bin when they reached the shore. This way, there would be zero waste. Being aware of leaving trash was one of the neat things I liked about scuba diving because most divers and boat crew were environmentally conscientious.

There were times when I was diving that I saw a piece of trash floating in the water. Worse, there were occasions when the sea life was entangled in a plastic bag. I attached a mesh bag to one of the D rings on my BCD so if I found garbage, I could pick it up.

A lot of times, what I would pick up would not be garbage but an item a fellow diver had dropped. In most cases, it was a go pro someone used to take videos. I always wondered why divers chose to hold onto to their cameras rather than clip them to their BCD. Later on, I would see someone post on one of the diving social media sites they lost a piece of their gear at one of the dive sites.

As I was pondering on the decisions of other divers, Aiden came up and sat down next to me.

"I'm sorry Drew was giving you a hard time about being low on air," he said.

"That's okay. Thanks for sticking up for me, and hopefully, I won't be the first one to be low on air for the second dive," I said.

"*Hola* Claire, hi Aiden," interrupted Miguel. He was holding a wooden cutting board with fresh pineapple and mango slices. "Would you guys like some fresh fruit?"

"Oh... that looks delicious!" I said looking at the fruit on the cutting board.

Aiden waved his hand in a gentlemanly fashion towards the fruit, indicating that I should take some pieces first.

"Thank you!" I reached toward the cutting board and grabbed three pieces of pineapple spears. The fruit was perfectly ripe and was so refreshing after the dive.

For a few minutes, both Aiden and I ate our snacks in silence as the boat sped towards the second dive location. For the second dive, Marcos asked the group where we wanted to go. Usually, the depth for the second dive was less than the first dive, but we wanted to do another deep dive, so we decided to dive the Santa Rosa Wall.

Diving the Santa Rosa Wall could be tricky because it sometimes had strong currents, and it would be important for everyone to stay together; otherwise, someone could get left behind quickly or the diver out in front could get way ahead of the group. As we neared the site and started to put back on our gear, Marcos briefed everyone the dive plan. We would be dropped off in the sandy part of the sea, which was about 60ft below sea level, and we would swim to the reef area where we would descend to 80ft.

From that depth, we would follow Marcos along the reef which was also called wall diving because on the other side of the reef was the open ocean where the bottom was a thousand feet or more. It sounded scary, but if you followed the guide at the correct depth, you wouldn't get lost and drift out into the open ocean. In addition to the beautiful coral formations, there were some great swim throughs, so we would do a multilevel dive.

When we got closer to the end of our dive, we should be drifting on top of the reef where we could see a wide range of fishes including barracudas. The first time I swam near one, I was amazed by their sleek shape and razor-sharp teeth. Even though the barracudas had no interest in me, I made sure to give the school of fishes a wide berth.

Shortly after Marcos finished the briefing, Raul cut the engine. This was a signal for the divers to walk to the back of the boat where Miguel would help us take a long stride into the water.

When Marcos and Carlos saw all eight of their divers were in the water, they signaled for everyone to descend to the sandy bottom. Once everyone reached the bottom, we swam perpendicular to the current towards the reef. We followed Marcos and Carlos over the top of the reef towards the open water. For this dive, Carlos was guiding me, Aiden, Ryan, and Peyton while Marcos was taking Drew and three other divers.

My group followed Carlos as he used his powerful flashlight to look in the crevices to find interesting sea creatures that were trying to hide from the predators in the food chain. With diving, I found sometimes you were able to see really neat things, but other times, you couldn't find any sea creatures. And today was one of those days. Although there were plenty of fishes in the sea, we couldn't find anything unusual to point out to each other. Still, I found it relaxing to just swim through the reef and listen to my breathing.

The dive time seemed to go by quickly, and this time, Ryan signaled to the group he was low on air. Since Drew had made such a commotion during the first dive about ascending early, Marcos and Carlos decided that if both groups did not have to come up together, then only one group would surface at a time. Therefore, Carlos signaled to me, Aiden, and Peyton we should follow Ryan to about fifteen feet to do our safety stop.

With the safety stop completed, we ascended to the surface to wait for Raul and the *Catalina* to pick us up. We didn't have to wait long because we heard Raul's voice in the distance.

"*Hola amigos*," shouted Raul from the boat in a sing song voice.

I swiveled my head towards the direction of the voice to see the *Catalina* was quickly approaching the area where we were floating. Once the captain cut the engine, the group swam towards the ladder one by one to be hauled up with our gear. This time I was the last person to climb the ladder, and before I was fully inside the boat, I heard voices below me.

It was Marcos' group that submerged out of the water. I heard a familiar voice say, "I had more air. I don't know why I couldn't have stayed down longer." I twisted my body around on the ladder in time to see Drew's irritated expression.

"*Señora* Tanaka reached her low air limit, and it's safer if we all came up as a group. If you did not come up when the rest of us did, you would have been the only one below," answered Marcos patiently. "I was also close to my low air limit as well," he added.

"Well, I guess I'm the only one who can really conserve air," Drew replied smugly.

"You were the only one using a 100 cubic feet tank," interjected Tom Tanaka. If all of us had larger tanks, we would have been able to stay down longer too.

"Well, you ALL should have paid extra like I did," smirked Drew.

Tom flared his nostrils. He was going to reply, but his wife grabbed onto his arm and shook her head. He bit back the retort he wanted to say.

Drew curled his lips in a sneer and said, "I thought so.'

Since there was no more that could be said to Drew to change his opinion, the rest of his group silently swam to the ladder to climb out of the water. What should have been a relaxing and fun day of diving was marred by Drew's behavior. Determined not to let his attitude affect me, I walked to the front of the boat and started to take off my wet suit. By this time, I was tired, and the wet suit was snug, so I had a hard time slipping the neoprene material over my shoulder.

"Hey, the wetsuit would come off a lot easier if you lost a few pounds," said a voice behind me.

I stopped tugging on the wetsuit and looked behind to see Drew standing a few inches away. I was shocked by what he just said to me. I narrowed my eyes and tried to think of a good comeback for Drew's rude remarks, but I couldn't think of anything without being just as mean as he was.

Wrestling silently in my head, I was trying to decide if I wanted to say the mean thought aloud when I heard Carlos say to Drew, "that was not a nice thing to say to Claire. You should apologize for being rude."

Drew looked surprised Carlos had called him out on his behavior. He stuttered, "it was just a joke!"

"It's not a joke to talk about someone's weight, and you know that," pressed Carlos. Drew looked stunned. Although he looked like he wanted to say something more, he glared at Carlos and walked away.

"*Gracias, Carlos!*" I said, but Carlos was still looking at Drew as he walked to the back of the boat. Judging by the expression on Carlos's expression, he took Drew's rude comment more personally than I did.

Carlos must have realized he was still staring at Drew, so he flashed a bright smile at me and said, "*de nada*. Here let me help you with your wetsuit."

With Carlos's help, I was able to easily get the wetsuit over my shoulders. When I told Carlos I would be able to manage with the rest of the suit, he nodded and smiled. With a wave, he walked to where Marcos was talking to Raul.

Although the *Catalina* was not a large boat, it had two levels. The top level was where the steering wheel was, and it had a ledge where Marcos and Carlos liked to sit and chat with Raul and Miguel as the boat chugged through the waves. I had a feeling if Drew weren't on the boat with the group, the dive crew would have chosen to sit with the divers. But given the fact Drew was so confrontational to everyone, I guessed the crew didn't want to have to play referee during the surface intervals.

Since the Santa Rosa Wall was close to the resort area, it didn't take the boat long to reach the pier. The *Catalina* moved towards the dock front end first. When the boat stopped, I was one of the first to get off. I took my equipment to the freshwater tank to rinse off the salt water. With my thoughts focused on cleaning my diving gear, I didn't see what the other people on the boat were doing, so I didn't see what happened to the guy that everyone in the group unanimously found disagreeable.

Chapter Eleven

I was by the plastic tub filled with fresh water rinsing out my scuba diving gear when I saw Drew walk into the dive shop. I thought he looked irate, but since that was a normal look for the guy, I didn't think too much about it and continued rinsing out my stuff.

"*Hola Claire, ¿Qué pasó?*" I looked up to see Carlos walking towards me with rental BCDs in each hand.

I waved and replied, "*nada, ¿y tú?*"

He smiled and shook his head, indicating that not much was going on as well.

"Did you enjoy the diving?" He asked as he set the BCDs down by the washbasin.

"Yes, it was wonderful! I was amazed how beautiful and clear the waters off of Cozumel are." I sighed in contentment as I thought back to the dives.

"You were lucky we had great weather, and we didn't have to close the port or have any of the dive sites be restricted." Carlos added.

That's true I thought. Scuba diving in the winter could be tricky because if the winds were too strong, the Mexican port authority would close off the Marina to small boats and thereby preventing access to the dive sites. It never happened to me, but I had heard stories about divers who showed up for a weeklong vacation to go diving but didn't get to go at all during the entire stay because of the weather conditions. I considered myself lucky I was able to spend time with my friends but also have a few hours during the day to do my favorite hobby.

As Carlos and I rinsed off our gear, we talked about the day's dive.

"I'm glad the water was so clear, but I'm disappointed I didn't see a shark or an eagle ray!" I gave a little pout. Carlos nodded and said, "well, sometimes the fish like to hide." He chuckled at his own joke. "You'll just have to keep coming back to Cozumel until you see everything." He teased and flashed his bright smile.

"I wish!" I exclaimed.

We both laughed, and I regretted I couldn't stay longer than our weekend trip. I wondered when the next time I could come back when my thoughts were interrupted by the slamming of the dive shop door.

"Whoa, Drew looks mad," I commented under my breath as I saw him stomp out of the dive shop back towards the boat pier.

"What do you think is wrong with him?" I debated whether I should call out to Drew, but I decided I wasn't that curious. He was probably still in a tiff because he didn't get extra time underwater when he had more air.

When I didn't hear a response back from Carlos, I looked at him and saw he had a dark look on his face.

"Is everything okay?" I asked.

"What? Oh yes, no problem," replied Carlos, but he didn't look okay.

I felt his answers were terse and was going to press further, but the dive shop door opened again, and the receptionist, Elena, waved at Carlos.

"Carlos, *señor Domínguez* wants to talk to you."

"I wonder why your boss wants to talk to you?" I glanced at Carlos again hoping he wasn't in trouble.

Carlos didn't answer, but he didn't look surprised the owner of the dive shop wanted to talk to him. In fact, he kind of looked resigned. I reached over and placed a hand on his shoulder.

"Are you sure you are okay?" I didn't like the look he had. Instead of answering my questions, he removed my hand from his shoulder and gently squeezed it before releasing it.

"I'm glad you enjoyed your dives today, and I hope you and your friends enjoy the rest of your time in Cozumel." With that, he left me staring after him as he walked towards the dive shop.

Chapter Twelve

"What the heck?" I said in surprise. I watched Carlos enter the dive shop with a dejected look on his face. I had no idea what was going on, but I would put money that Drew had something to do with it. I wanted to go after him, but I thought it would make things worse, so I told myself I would ask Carlos what happened when I saw him again.

I finished rinsing off my scuba gear with fresh water and packed it in my mesh bag. As I walked back to my room, I thought how it was odd that Carlos was called into the office. I hoped he wasn't going to get in trouble for anything.

"Hey Claire!"

"Oh, hey guys!" To my surprise, Aiden and Ryan were by the hotel pool bar having a drink, and they motioned for me to join them.

"Do you want something to drink," Ryan asked as he pointed to the beers he and Aiden were drinking.

"Sure, I'll take whatever you guys are having. Thanks!" I said to Ryan as he walked over to the bartender to get my drink.

"How much longer are you staying in Cozumel?" Aiden asked.

My face flushed as I met his gaze. I thought I might be imagining things, but it seemed as though Aiden was flirting with me.

I twirled a strand of my hair. "I'm supposed to leave the island on Sunday. I think I mentioned it before, but I'm here for a bachelorette party. I signed up to dive because I didn't want to hang out by the pool all day."

I didn't mention I was trying to avoid spending time in the vicinity of one of the bridesmaids. "Since there are six of us girls, I figured I wouldn't be missed too much if I stole a few hours early in the morning while everyone was still asleep to go diving."

"What about you? How many more days do you have left," I asked Aiden.

"Ryan and I have three more days left on our vacation," he replied. "We were roommates in law school, but we practice law in different cities, so every few years we try to have a reunion to catch up on life. I'm usually not a fan of Ryan's adventure vacations, but I will say this is by far the best trip he has put together so far."

"See I told you that you would love scuba diving!" exclaimed Ryan. He came back from the bar and handed me the beer. I looked down at the bottle of *Modelo* and wondered why I agreed to a beer because I didn't like the taste of it. I usually order wine or cocktails if I went out. I guess was so flattered the guys asked me to talk with them that I didn't think about what I wanted to drink.

I should have gotten a *mojito* but not wanting to be rude, I took a cautious sip of my beer and decided it wasn't too bad. It had a light citrus taste. I took another sip.

"Okay, you were right," Aiden raised both hands and shrugged in defeat.

"You should have heard him when I suggested that we get our scuba diving licenses."

"What did he say?" I asked Ryan. I was curious to find out how much Aiden was into diving.

"At first-nothing. There was silence at the end of the line." Ryan laughed as he recalled their phone conversation.

"That's because you caught me off-guard," Aiden said. "You didn't give me time to process what you said."

"That's true, and you did warm up to the idea when I said we didn't have to do our check-out dives in the Bay Area. Instead, we could go someplace warmer," Ryan added.

"Yup, what really sold me on the idea was when you told me we could come to Cozumel to do our check-out dives. I always wanted to come here, and now I'm glad I did." When Aiden said the last part, he looked at me.

I blushed, and I tried to act nonchalantly as I said, "I'm really glad you guys came." I took another sip from the bottle. The beer was pretty good. I think I was drinking the wrong type of beer all this time.

"Where do you practice law? I asked Aiden.

Maybe it was the beer that gave me confidence, but I was pleasantly surprised how well I was holding up the conversation. By now, I expected to say something about finding my friends and leaving the guys. Yet, somehow, I was still there talking to them.

I also noticed the more time I spent talking to Aiden, the more he became attractive to me. What stood out was that when he spoke to me, his eyes were focused on me and not wandering around the room. There was nothing I disliked more than when the person I was talking to kept glancing around at other people while I spoke. It made me feel like what I had to say was not important. But Aiden held my gaze while we talked .

"My law office is in Mountain View, and Ryan practices in Phoenix."

"Mountain View- is that near San Jose?"

"Yes, that's right. Have you ever been there?" Aiden asked, surprised that I heard of the place.

"No, but my best friend lives in San Francisco, so I know where it is," I explained.

"Oh, do you also live in the Bay area? We should get together sometime." Aiden said as he took a few steps closer to me.

"Actually, I teach English overseas, but my best friend is getting married in San Francisco next week, so I am staying with her until her wedding. And then, I'm going to dog sit while Julia and her soon to be husband go on their honeymoon,"

I knew I was rambling, but I was getting a little unnerved by Aiden's close presence. My face felt warm. Then, to my chagrin, I blurted out "speaking of Julia, I should probably go find my friends."

Aiden looked baffled at my statement.

Argh! Well- there it was, I thought ruefully. I made the exit speech I was so worried about making. Although I wanted to kick myself for being so awkward and ending the conversation so abruptly, I realized I probably should go find my friends because I hadn't talked to them since our dinner last night.

Aiden seemed to have recovered from his earlier confusion and said smoothly, "Of course! You should go find your friends but let me give you my number before you go up to your room." He then quickly headed to the bar to see if he could get a piece of paper and a pen from the bartender.

Despite the awkward ending, I was impressed I had a decent conversation with a good-looking guy for at least ten minutes before I ruined it. Although, *it wasn't as polished as Annisa would have made it,* I thought as the self-doubt crept in.

I was so absorbed mentally replaying my conversation with Aiden that I was startled to hear a scream from the pier.

Chapter Thirteen

"What was that noise?" I jumped up from the bar stool to see who or what had made the sound.

"I don't know, exclaimed Aiden. He had overhead my question when he hurried back with a pen and a piece of paper. "It sounded like it came from the pier." We both looked in the direction of the beach. We saw there was a flurry of activity around the dive boat.

With a few other people from the bar, we rushed to the pier to see what happened. I gasped when I got closer to the pier. I didn't expect to see Elena, the Scuba Mar receptionist, standing over a body that looked very similar to Drew. Although I couldn't see the face, I could see a glimpse of the red and white scuba flag tattoo on the person's arm. I was pretty sure it was him because over the past couple of days, I hadn't seen anyone else with a tattoo like that.

"Is he okay," asked Tom Tanaka. He and Margaret followed Aiden and me to the pier.

"He's not breathing. I think he is dead," answered Elena. She looked like she was going to cry but the enormity of the situation kept her emotions from showing. Elena added woodenly, "I was locking the door to the building when I saw *señor* Drew lying down on the dock. I thought he might be injured, so I went over to help him. However, when I called his name and tried to shake him, he didn't answer. I got down to see if he was breathing, but I couldn't feel any air coming from his nose or his mouth."

Elena confirmed my suspicion that the person was Drew.

"Who screamed?" asked Aiden.

"I did," said Elena. "When I noticed he needed emergency care, I called for help, and then I proceeded to give him CPR. You know everyone at Scuba Mar is CPR certified, but after several minutes, I realized he was not responding, and I screamed in frustration."

Just as the receptionist finished telling us what happened, the police and first responders arrived at the scene. I could see them running towards the pier.

When the emergency crew got to the pier, the police pushed us away from the body, but they didn't make us leave the area. There were still a lot of people huddled together watching the medics try to revive Drew.

"I can't believe Drew is dead!" said Margaret. She was dismayed seeing Drew's body. I remembered Drew and the Tanakas had a verbal spat while we were diving this morning. Poor Margaret was probably replaying the scene in her head. I reached out to Margaret and patted her arm sympathetically.

Although I didn't wish death upon anyone including an annoying guy like Drew, I was surprised frankly that someone from the group hadn't tried to push him off the boat. After I finished this thought, I felt guilty.

I watched the Mexican police walk around the resort and talk to the hotel manager and the employees who had shown up after they saw the people rush toward the pier. The police also interviewed the dive company employees. As the police walked around talking to everyone, the resort guests wandered around the crime scene taking photos of the covered-up body and also selfies of the scene. I was positive some of these people were going to post the horrendous episode on their social media account as a cheap way of garnering more followers. It was sad that someone's tragedy was another's way of entertainment as though these two incidents were divorced.

When a young man with a selfie-stick jostled for more room with another woman to get the best shot of the body and himself, the police decided that was enough, and shooed away the bystanders. When the crowd dispersed, the only people left on the scene were the people from the boat that Drew was on and the police. Even though we didn't know him well, we wanted to know what happened. The uniformed police continued to walk through the area for a few more minutes taking pictures and notes until two people wearing suits approached the police officers.

I saw these two people compare notes with the uniformed police and then looked around to see who they needed to interview. Judging from their stern expressions and demeanor, I assumed these two people were also from the police department. I didn't know much about the police, but based on the TV crime shows I watched, the two people in suits were detectives.

As the detectives scanned the remaining small crowd at the crime scene, I wondered if they would interview me. However, one of the detectives who was a tall woman with her brunette hair coiled in a severe bun on top of her head looked past me to where Aiden and Ryan were standing looking in disbelief.

"*Disculpe, señores*. My name is Detective Martinez, and this is Detective Rojas. Can one of you gentlemen tell me if you spoke to the victim at all today?"

"Yes, we all did," said Aiden. "It was hard to NOT to talk to

Drew because he inserted himself in every conversation even though we tried to switch topics. It appeared he was an expert in everything and had to tell us how much he knew about whatever we were talking about."

"It was maddening," Ryan added. "Every time Drew opened his big mouth, I shot him dirty looks, but the guy was able to ignore even the most obvious signals."

The detectives looked taken back at the way Aiden and Ryan described their interaction with Drew. The guys seemed to realize that, and Ryan swiftly made amends.

"What I meant to say was Drew could be a little pushy."

"Look, we're sorry that Drew died, but you got to know he wasn't well-liked," Peyton chimed in from beside me. I was so focused on the detectives I didn't see her coming to stand next to me.

Turning her stern gaze around, Detective Martinez said, "*Perdóname señorita*, who are you?"

"My name is Peyton Barnes, and I was on the boat with Drew this morning along with the guys you just questioned. I'm also staying at the resort with my parents."

"*Gracias*" said the detective. Can you tell me if anyone argued with the victim or saw anything suspicious?

Before Peyton could answer the detective's question, Aiden spoke up.

"Well- Aiden hesitated. We kind of all argued with Drew in a way, but that didn't mean we killed him. We just wanted him to go away. Which, I guess it's hard to do when we are stuck on a moving vessel."

"How about anything suspicious or out of place," asked Detective Rojas this time.

"No, I didn't see anything out of place" Aiden replied, but I saw Ryan scrunching his face as if he looked as though he saw something. Detective Martinez also picked up Ryan's expression because she said, "*Sí, señor*?"

Ryan still looked conflicted. The detective noted Ryan's dilemma and asked him again a little more forcefully. "*Señor*, if you saw something-anything, it could be important to figure out who could have done this terrible thing to your friend."

"Uh... he wasn't my friend." Ryan looked guilty about his statement, but it was the truth. I had to agree with Ryan. Drew did not endear himself to anyone on the boat. Ryan cleared his throat, and said, "after we unloaded our stuff off the boat, I saw one of our dive masters, Carlos, talking to Drew. It looked like they were arguing, and although I couldn't hear what they were saying, it seemed that Carlos was mad at Drew. When Drew started to walk away, I saw Carlos grab his arm."

"What happened next *señor*?" asked Detective Rojas who was writing down what Ryan was saying carefully in his small, green waterproof notepad.

"Well, when Carlos grabbed Drew's arm, he just jerked it out of Carlos' grasp and walked away. I think he said something, but I couldn't hear what he said because I was too far away."

"Did either one of you also see this argument?" asked Detective Martinez.

Aiden and Peyton shook their heads. When they didn't make a motion to speak, the detectives concluded there was nothing else to add to their investigation. I think they were disappointed by the lack of information judging from their expressions.

"*Gracias*" said the two detectives. For some reason, the detective skipped me as they went around and handed their business cards to the guys and Peyton. Then, they left with the parting request, "if you remember anything else, please do not hesitate to contact either one of us. We are so sorry about your *amigo*. Have a good day."

"He wasn't our friend," Ryan muttered.

I didn't know why Ryan kept insisting Drew wasn't our friend, but I thought it was because he was still processing seeing a dead body. Slowly, the guys came out of their trance, and without saying goodbye, they started to walk back to the hotel lobby where I assumed they were going to the elevator to head back to their rooms. Either that, or they were headed to the hotel lobby bar to down a few *mojitos* and try to forget what happened to Drew. I was going to follow the guys back to the resort, but I noticed Peyton was still next to me. She seemed rooted in place, so I turned to her to see if she was okay.

"How are you doing?" I asked.

"It's so surreal. Earlier today, I was so annoyed by Drew I actually wished he was dead. Now that he is dead, I'm wondering if my wish had anything to do with his death," Peyton whispered. Her face was white as a sheet. She looked like she was going to faint.

"I doubt it," I said to sooth Peyton. "The guy was a jerk, and I'm sure that you were not the only one who wished him gone. In fact, I think I had a few uncharitable thoughts about him as well on our return ride home when he commented that if I lost a few pounds, it would be easier to get my arms out of my wetsuit!"

I cringed as I was reminded of what had happened earlier in the day when I was trying to get my wetsuit off so I could warm up in the sun. Even though the wetsuit kept me toasty in the water, out of the water, wearing a damp wet suit was chilling.

I turned back to Peyton to see how she was doing. "Yeah," said Peyton. "I guess that's true." She didn't look convinced that she didn't have anything to do with Drew's death.

"Why don't you go back to your room and rest?" I suggested kindly when I saw Peyton looked like she was going to start crying. *Uh-oh*, I thought. Peyton's crying would make me uncomfortable. I hated to admit it, but I get squirmy whenever anyone cries in front of me because I never know what to do or say. I gave Peyton a hug and patted her back. She hugged me back and then pulled away.

"Okay, that's a good idea," spoke Peyton softly. Dazed by witnessing Drew's dead body, we walked silently back to our rooms at the resort.

Chapter Fourteen

"What?!" Drew's dead?" Julia yelled. Her eyes widen in disbelief. "Wow. I can't believe it! Do you think someone killed him?" Although Julia didn't go on any of the diving trips during this bachelorette weekend, she heard all about how conceited he was from me.

Plus, she saw the annoying dude in action during his clumsy attempts to try to pick up women in the hotel lobby bar including some of Julia's friends. It didn't work. The only person who thought Drew's cheesy jokes were charming was Annisa.

"Well, I'm sure the police will eventually figure out what happened to Drew, and if anyone killed him. I'm so glad we're leaving this place on Sunday, so we can get back to normal," Julia added.

I frowned. I thought Julia was being too dismissive about the situation, but it was probably because she didn't spend much time with Drew over the last two days. Although I didn't like Drew, being around him these few days humanized him in a way that Julia was not able to understand.

I just shrugged my shoulders and said "hmmm… I guess you're right."

"So, who were you talking to at the bar," asked Julia switching the topic from one guy to another.

"Who?" I pretended I didn't know what Julia was talking about.

"Oh, come on! The good-looking guy you were talking to at the pool bar. He seemed like he was really into you." Julia said in exasperation as she rolled her eyes.

"You think so?"

"Yes! I'm positive he's interested in you." Julia declared and walked to me so she could face me. "So- who is he?"

"He's name is Aiden," I admitted. "He's one of the divers I dove with. He and his friend Ryan are friends from their law school days and every few years, they try to go on vacation together and catch up on things."

"Really," said Julia. She looked at me intently and gave me a knowing smile when I answered her in a breezy fashion as though I was not interested in the subject. "Hmm…you certainly know more about the guy who you claim that you are not interested in."

"So, where is he from?" Julia pressed. She was not going to let me get off so easily.

"Uh- he has his practice in Mountain View," I replied grudgingly. I didn't want to continue talking about Aiden because I didn't want to make him sound more important than he was because I was sure nothing was going to come out of it.

But Julia didn't think so and said, "that's only an hour away from San Francisco!" She was way too excited about a guy I just met. "Maybe you can ask him to be your date to my wedding."

"Whoa! Let's not get too ahead of ourselves," I answered as I saw the direction Julia was heading. "We just met, and after witnessing a dead body, I doubt he wants to be reminded of this unpleasant incident."

"Did you get his number?" Julia wouldn't back off.

"Yes, but again, he gave me his info BEFORE we saw Drew's dead body, so I think that negates his previous interest in me."

"You don't know that, and you should definitely give him a call."

Trying to change the subject, I said, "hey-look at the time! We should get ready for dinner. The girls are meeting us downstairs in the lobby to go to dinner." For tonight's dinner, we decided not to eat at the resort and try a local restaurant. Even though the resort had three all-inclusive meal options which were fantastic, we wanted to try a local restaurant before we left for home. We decided on a small but highly recommended restaurant called *Albertos*. One of the bartenders the other girls got to know well these past two days laying out by the pool mentioned *Albertos* had the best fish tacos in Cozumel.

Anticipating flaky white fish meat served with tangy salsa spurred me into action.

"I get the first shower," I called out heading to the bathroom.

"That's fine," Julia said and added, "But don't think the topic of our previous conversation is over. I'm going to text the others to let them know we'll meet them down in the lobby in thirty minutes. Do you think that will be enough time to get ready?"

"You better make it an hour."

"Why?" asked Julia doubtful about the increase in time. "All we have to do is change from our swimsuits to some shorts and t-shirts"

"Just put on shorts and t-shirts- are you kidding?" I said mockingly. "There is no way Annisa is going to ever just throw on some shorts and a t-shirt. Glamour girl has to put on the whole production." I waved my hand over my face to make the point.

Julia covered her mouth with her hand to smother a laugh

and nodded at my description. While we all skipped wearing makeup during our weekend trip to Cozumel, Annisa insisted on wearing foundation and fixing her hair which I thought was a huge waste of time since the weather was humid even for December.

"That's true. I should tell the girls to meet downstairs in an hour and half," laughed Julia.

"No, an hour should be sufficient. I'm betting it'll take forty-five minutes, but we'll give her an extra fifteen minutes to make a grand entrance." Julia and I laughed as we thought of Annisa striding out of the elevator asking innocently if she was late while we all looked at her exasperatingly.

I remembered a few years ago, before Julia met her fiancé, Julia, Annisa, Michelle, and I went to New York City for New Year's Eve. Even though everyone was clear we had to meet in the lobby at 7:30pm so we could get an Uber ride to Times Square without paying a "busy time" surcharge, Annisa came down at 8:30pm. At that point, it took another hour to get a car that would take us downtown. We could have walked, but we decided to dress up for the occasion, so we weren't wearing appropriate walking shoes.

By the time we got an Uber to take us downtown, we had to pay triple what it would have cost us had we left at the time we had originally agreed upon. What made it more irritating was that Annisa said we should have left earlier so we could have gotten closer to the stage where the performers were. I almost said something snarky about the cause of our delay, but Julia and Michelle anticipated my response and jabbed me with their elbows to keep me quiet when they sensed that I was going to say something. The effect of their elbows hitting on both sides of my ribs caused me to lose interest in saying something mean to Annisa. In the end, it was probably good that I didn't say anything because we had a great time despite paying extra to get downtown.

Freshly showered, Julia and I smelled like a fragrance store. When we were in college, one of the splurges we made was to buy fancy soaps and lotion even though we could have saved a bundle using drugstore brands. But, the scent of spiced vanilla always brought a smile to my face, and it was so relaxing. On the other hand, Julia favored fruity flavors. In addition to the lotions, Julia bought candles of the same fragrance from the store and lit them in our dorm room. As a result, the little 300 square feet room always smelled like a fruit stand.

With one last look to make sure all the valuables were locked in the hotel's closet safe, I picked up my key and walked behind Julia, so I was the last one out the door. Earlier in our college rooming period, I found that Julia did not always close the door securely. One time during our senior year, I came back to the dorm to find the door wide open. Apparently, Julia didn't shut the door tight, and a breeze pushed the door open. At first, it appeared that nothing was taken or disturbed, but later, I found my hidden stash of M & Ms was missing. I never found out who took them, but taking the candy was better than having someone steal my mountain bike that was leaning against the wall next to the door.

When we reached the elevator, Julia pushed the elevator button for the lobby. While we waited for the elevator to come down, Emma walked towards us.

"Hey Em, how's it going?"

"I'm alright. I just woke up from a nap a few minutes ago, so I'm a little groggy. I'm also probably dehydrated," said Emma. Like us, she was dressed casually in a short sundress.

"Nothing that some water and margarita can't fix," Julia assured her friend. "Where's Annisa?"

Emma looked at us and widened her eyes. Emma hadn't known Annisa as long as Julia and me, but she had been to enough events where Annisa also attended to get a feel for her personality. Because I got to room with Julia for being her maid of honor and best friend and all the other girls not wanting to room with Annisa, Emma got stuck with her on this trip.

Thankfully, this arrangement worked out. Emma was a chill person and could tolerate Annisa's dramatic behavior. She either dismissed Annisa's comments, or she would say something sarcastic that usually went over Annisa's head. I loved having Emma around. With her dry British sense of humor, it kept me from strangling Annisa I didn't think Julia would appreciate it if I took out one of her bridesmaids.

The elevator pinged, and its door opened. Michelle and Olivia who were rooming together on the floor above us were already inside.

We smiled at each other and made room for everyone to fit in the elevator. Fortunately, the elevator was quite roomy and there was plenty of space. We chatted as we rode the lift down to the lobby. I was listening to Michelle and Olivia debate whether they wanted to order a *mojito* or a margarita. Both sounded really good to them.

"Why don't you order both?" I said logically. We weren't driving and ordering two drinks didn't seem unreasonable.

The girls shrugged and said, "yeah, that's a good idea." We continued to walk and talk until we reached the rattan benches where we could sit and wait for Annisa.

"Hey, isn't that one of your guides from the diving company?" asked Julia. I looked over at the direction Julia was talking about and saw that it was indeed someone I knew.

"Yeah, that's Carlos! I wonder why he is talking to the two detectives." It was odd the Mexican detectives were still at the hotel. Maybe they had left and come back, but I was especially interested to know why they were talking to Carlos. Before I could think of an answer, I saw Detective Rojas reach for his handcuffs. ,The next thing I knew, Carlos was handcuffed, and Detective Martinez was leading him out of the hotel lobby.

"What! Why are they taking Carlos? Do the police think he had something to do with Drew's murder?" I asked my group.

"I don't know," said Julia. "Why don't you ask the hotel manager what's going on."

"Good idea! Let me go find the manager," I said, forgetting we were supposed to go out to dinner.

"Right now? We're leaving for the restaurant," Julia called out in dismay. At that moment we heard a woman's voice call out "hey girls, are we ready?" I turned around to see Annisa strolling up to the group as though everyone was late, and she was the one patiently waiting for us. As usual, she looked gorgeous. Her hair was blown out into big curly waves, and her face was perfectly made up. She was also wearing a floral maxi dress that accented her slender figure and wedge sandals that made her several inches taller.

I looked at my own outfit. I thought I looked cute wearing a light pink romper with flip flops, but compared to Annisa, I looked like a kid going out with her glamorous sister.

I sighed and instead of getting annoyed at Annisa and saying something snippy, I told the girls, "Why don't you go ahead. I'm going to find out why the police took Carlos."

Julia bit her bottom lip in frustration and said, "alright, but we'll see you in a little bit-right?" Julia knew from my expression that when I became focused on finding out what happened, I wouldn't let it go until I found the answers.

"We'll see you in a few minutes-right, Claire?" Julia put her hand on my forearm to get my attention. She wanted to be sure I wasn't going to leave them.

"Yeah, of course. I'll be right behind you guys. Save me a seat," I said. Julia looked unconvinced, but the other girls were ready to move on to dinner, so she gave me a look that said you better not ditch us. I silently communicated back by nodding and opened my eyes really wide which meant, *I won't*. I gave

Julia a pat on the arm to reassure her, and I said, "Give me five minutes, and I'll meet you at the restaurant."

Julia nodded and with a wave, she followed the girls as they walked down the stone paved driveway careful not to trip over the uneven stones. Before they were even out of sight, I turned to find the manager of the resort.

Chapter Fifteen

"*Disculpe*-excuse me," I said to the woman at the front desk. "Where can I find the manager?"

"*Señor Ramirez* is by the palm tree over there talking to those two gentlemen" said Lupe, the front desk clerk. I looked to where Lupe was pointing at and saw a tall man with a dark mustache talking to Marcos and another person from the dive shop. I figured the other person Marcos and the manager were talking to was the dive shop owner. They were probably discussing what had happened to Carlos.

I walked over to the men and said, "*Perdónme*."

Although Marcos was used to me speaking Spanish, the other two men were surprised.

"*Sí, Señorita*. What can we help you with? Are you lost?" said the man who was the manager.

"No, I am not lost. I just wanted to know if you knew why the police took away Carlos. You don't think he had anything to do with what happened this afternoon on the pier do you?" I asked. The three men exchanged glances, and it was Marcos who spoke.

"Claire, the police had some questions for Carlos, so they wanted to bring him into the precinct for questioning."

"But, why did they put him in handcuffs?" I pressed the men because it didn't seem necessary to put Carlos in handcuffs if they only wanted to question him. They must have had a reason.

"Well, we're not sure, but it appears the police have some evidence connecting Carlos with *señor* Drew's death," said the man who I assumed was the dive shop owner.

I looked at the owner. He was very tall, at least six-four I guessed. He had short dark hair in the back, but the front part was long and swept over his head where an ample amount of hair gel kept it in place. Although I had seen him around the dive shop, I had never spoken to him. "What's the evidence the police have?" I asked not liking the sound of things.

"*No sé,*" the dive shop owner shrugged. For a guy who just had one of his employees taken into custody, he seemed pretty unconcerned, which made me a little suspicious.

"Are you going down to the precinct to bail Carlos out?" I asked the dive shop owner.

"Unfortunately, I had to let Carlos go," the owner said.

"What! You fired, Carlos? Why?" I said in alarm. Now, it made more sense why the dive shop owner seemed detached from Carlos' arrest. I blew out a frustrated breath. First, the police took Carlos away in handcuffs. Then I found out there was evidence linking Carlos to the death. And now the ultimate insult, Carlos was fired right before he was arrested. My head was spinning with the information I heard.

"I didn't want to fire Carlos because he was an excellent employee for over five years, and I never had any troubles with him before with any of the customers." To his credit, the owner looked upset he had to fire Carlos. But I was not mollified.

"Then, what was the reason you HAD to let one of your best employees go?" I demanded.

"Well, after the last morning dive, one of the guests came to me and complained about Carlos. He said Carlos grabbed his arm and made menacing threats to him. The guest said if I didn't let Carlos go, then he was going to write a terrible review on several different travel websites about our company. And well, I have to look out for all my employees." The owner made it sound like he didn't have a choice, but I wasn't convinced.

If I was a betting person, I would bet that when I saw Drew entering the dive shop this afternoon, it was to complain to the owner about Carlos, and that's why he got fired. That was why he looked so irate.

The feeling of annoyance at the dead man was creeping in again, but I reminded myself that even if Drew had caused my friend to get fired, he still didn't deserve to die.

I sighed and thanked the men for their answers and walked back toward the lobby. I didn't feel hungry, but I knew I had to meet up with the rest of the group at *Alberto's*. Otherwise, Julia would never forgive me.

Deep in thought, I walked to the restaurant which was just a few blocks away. However, as I started to cross the driveway to the sidewalk, I didn't see a taxi that was pulling up to the waiting concierges.

"*Cuidado señorita!*" one of the concierges yelled.

"Wha..oh, sorry!" I needed to focus on getting to the restaurant alive so the police did not have to come back and investigate my death from crossing the driveway and not paying attention to traffic. For the rest of the way, I did my best to concentrate on walking to the restaurant.

A few minutes later, I arrived at the entrance of the eatery. *Alberto's* restaurant was one of those restaurants that didn't have a permanent store front. Instead, it had a rolling, metal door Alberto pulled up when he opened the restaurant for the day's business. As a result, the entire front of the restaurant facing the street was open. At the front was an elderly man sitting next to a stand which turned out to be Alberto himself.

"*Buenas noches señorita*," said Alberto. Can I help you?"

"*Sí, señor*. I'm looking for a large group of women that should have arrived about ten-fifteen minutes ago," I said as I craned my head around looking for my friends.

"Ah yes. The lovely *señoritas* are sitting at a table on the patio overlooking the beach. Go ahead and go back to the patio," said Alberto tilting his head in the direction of the water.

"*Muchas gracias.*"

As I walked towards the back of the restaurant which opened to the beach front, I could hear *mariachi* music playing loudly in the background. During my multiple trips to Mexico, I had gotten to love listening to *mariachi*. I started to sway side to side to the upbeat music as I walked toward my group when Julia spotted me. She waved her hand towards a chair that she saved next to her. She looked relieved to see I hadn't abandoned them.

I smiled gratefully and thought to myself that even though we weren't as close as we once were, Julia still considered me as her best friend.

"So, what did you find out?" Julia asked as I eased down on the chair.

"Not much, unfortunately. The dive shop owner told me the police may have evidence connecting Carlos to what happened, but he didn't know what it was. He also told me he fired Carlos because one of the guests complained about him."

"Do you know who it was that complained about Carlos?" asked Emma. She was sitting across from me and overhead my explanation to Julia.

"The dive shop owner didn't say who it was, but I saw Drew go into the dive shop when we came back from the last dive of the day, and he didn't look happy. I think he was the one that complained about Carlos," I explained.

"Do you mean the dead guy was the one who complained about your friend?" asked Olivia from the far end of the table. By this time, all the girls were listening to my explanation.

"Wait, wasn't he the guy that was flirting with Annisa the other night?" Emma pointed out the connection.

Annisa was about to eat a chip, but she put it down when she heard us talking about Drew.

Annisa looked horrified when she realized that Emma was right, but she didn't know what to say. She kept opening and closing her mouth trying to find words. She looked like a fish out of the water. I actually felt bad for her.

"I think it was Drew, but I'm not sure," I said again. "I just know after Drew stormed out of the dive shop, Carlos was summoned by Elena, the receptionist, to talk to the owner. I really hope the police is mistaken about the evidence, and they let Carlos go free."

"*Señorita*, can I get you something to drink?" A young waitress came up to our table as I finished talking.

I didn't need a menu to know what I wanted to drink. "Yes, I will have a margarita," I said.

"*Excelente.* I will bring your drink shortly, and then I will take your order," said the waitress.

"*Bueno, gracias.*" I looked around the table, and I asked if they had ordered food already. The ladies nodded, and then I noticed that they were drinking *mojitos* and snacking on fried *tortillas* and fresh *guacamole*. "Oh, I guess I should have ordered the *mojito* then" I said as I thought about my margarita order.

"Don't worry about it, Claire," said Emma. We decided we all wanted to get two drinks tonight, and we decided to order *mojitos* first."

"Okay, that works for me. I'll order a *mojito* after I finish the margarita." As soon as I mentioned my drink, the waitress magically appeared beside me with a large, wide-rimmed margarita glass full of a light greenish golden liquid.

"Ooh...this looks delicious!" I gushed as I reached for the drink.

The waitress grinned and said, "*sí,* I think you will enjoy this. Our margaritas are our house specialty made with a *tequila* that was produced especially for *Alberto's.*"

"Really?" chorused the girls.

"*Sí,* the owner has relatives that live in *Jalisco* where they grow agave plants." The tequila they make for *Albertos* is not the same brand they sell to the stores, but it is a special blend they make just for the family," explained the waitress.

"Wow, that's so cool!" exclaimed Michelle. "Now, I want to visit *Jalisco*!"

The waitress smiled at Michelle's remark, and then asked what I wanted to eat. I told the waitress I wanted to try *Alberto's* fish tacos to which the waitress also mentioned that it was also a house special.

"I feel like I hit the food jackpot!" I pumped my fist in the air.

"Well, you would know about hitting the food jackpot. Wouldn't you?" interjected Annisa.

The sympathetic feeling I had for her earlier passed away, but I was so pleased I ordered the house specials I ignored the pointed remark Annisa made towards my weight. Or least I thought was aimed at my weight. While everyone in Julia's party was thin, I was the only one that wasn't built like a model.

While the other girls fretted about how they looked in their bikinis, I rarely bothered to look in the mirror. I came to the conclusion a long time ago I would never be a model and accepted my chunkiness. I referred to the extra rolls on the back as my floatation devices.

As we waited for our food, I went back deep into my own thoughts while munching on fresh *guacamole* and chips. I tried to recall if there was a time when Carlos was seen talking to Drew, and except for the one time that Carlos stood up for me when Drew made a comment about my weight, I had a hard time coming up with an instance that the two men were alone together because Carlos, like the rest of us in the diving group, had tried to avoid Drew as much as possible.

I remembered one time when Drew came up to Marcos and "tried" to give him pointers on how to adjust the aluminum weights on his belt for the best buoyancy. Marcos just looked at Drew like he was a simple child and nodded in agreement. Although the diving crew earned money from the dive store operator, it wasn't much. The majority of the money the crew made was from the gratuity the divers gave to them after each diving trip. Therefore, the crew depended on the generosity of the guests and could not afford to offend them.

I took a big drink of my margarita, and I wondered, *what am I missing?*

Chapter Sixteen

S tuffed from all the decadent food and slightly tipsy from the strong drinks, we walked back to the resort hotel. At the lobby, the girls decided to have one more drink at the hotel bar before they went to their rooms. This decision was also based on the sighting of some cute guys going into the bar. By the way Michelle and Olivia glanced at the men and then each other, I could tell that they were interested in talking to them. But instead of following the rest of the girls to the lobby bar, I veered off towards the elevator. I almost got to the elevator when I felt a tug on my arm.

"Claire! Where are you going?" I turned around and saw Julia next to me.

"Did you say something?" I didn't see Julia following me because I was preoccupied by my own thoughts.

"Earth to Claire! Yes, I called your name several times. I finally had to chase after you," Julia said exasperatedly.

"Oh, sorry. What did you want?"

"I asked where you were going. Are you coming to have drinks with us at the bar?" asked Julia. I thought about the question for a second before I answered her.

"Actually, I'm going back to our room. I'm a little tired from this morning's dives." I put on a show of yawning and stretching my arms over my head.

"You're probably tired from diving and being in the sun. Plus, I'm sure seeing the dead guy didn't help. Listen- I shouldn't be more than an hour. I really don't want to have another drink, but I want to spend more time with Michelle and Olivia before they leave for Seattle."

While the rest of the girls lived in the Bay area, Michelle and Olivia lived and worked in Seattle. I didn't technically live in the Bay area either, but I was going to stay with Julia until her wedding because I was in-between teaching jobs. I was also going to pet sit Grumpy while Julia and her soon to be husband go on their honeymoon.

Grumpy was a sweet dog that loved to cuddle with people. Whenever someone sat on the couch, he would take his blanket and jump on the couch and arrange himself right next to the person. When he was in position, usually saddled next to the leg, he would flip the blanket over his head and settle down for a nap.

Julia's mom, Sumin, was watching Grumpy at the family home in San Mateo. Julia's mom didn't want to go back and forth in the Bay area traffic to take care of Grumpy, so she brought the dog to live with her and Julia's dad at their house while we were in Cozumel. At first, Julia's dad was not happy about the situation, but like most people who met Grumpy, he was charmed by the dog's blanket trick. Yesterday when Julia FaceTimed her parents to check on Grumpy, she saw he was sitting next to her dad under his blanket while her dad was watching the local news. Another Grumpy convert.

When I got to the door of my room, I searched in my purse for the keycard. Every time I rummaged through my bag, I thought about how I should be more organized. My travel purse resembled a bottomless pit. Somewhere inside the bag was a wallet, sunglasses, sunscreen, lip balm and lip gloss, a hand sanitizer bottle, and a travel size bottle of hand lotion. If that was all that was in the bag, I could have probably found the key more easily, but there were also various wadded up receipts and napkins.

"Oh, I should have put the stupid key in the wallet since that would have been the easiest thing to grab from the purse," I mumbled in the dim hall light. It was a good thing the hotel was safe because the time it took to find the keycard, I could have been robbed.

In frustration, I dumped everything out of my messy bag on the hall floor. After sifting through the clumped items, I finally touched the smooth plastic card with my fingers. With a triumphant sweep of my hand, I took the key card and inserted it into the door lock. A second later, the light on the door lock turned green from red, and I twisted the metal handle to open the door. I was greeted with the cool air from the air-conditioned room.

Although I didn't want to admit it at the time of booking the hotel rooms, I was grateful that Annisa insisted on reserving rooms at a resort that had air conditioning. Initially, I wasn't sure if the extra one hundred dollars a night was worth having air conditioning in the room, but now I had to concede that she was right. This December was unusually humid in Cozumel, and it would have been uncomfortable trying to go to sleep at night without air conditioning. But I was sure sleep was not the reason why Annisa insisted on it. She probably wanted air conditioning in order to keep the makeup from melting from her perfectly applied face and to keep her hair from frizzing out. I thought uncharitably.

Not wanting to dwell on Anissa further, I brought my attention back to the room. I had intended to pack my scuba stuff for tomorrow's dive, but I was distracted by the sea view when I looked out the window. It automatically reminded me of the scuba diving trip earlier today and what happened to Carlos. I just met Carlos, but for some reason I felt a connection to him, and during the boat rides back to the resort, I got to know him a little.

We talked about how he got into scuba diving. I found out that Carlos started diving when he was fifteen years old in Cancun where he grew up. His family owned a small *taqueria* next to a local dive shop. As a child, he would hang outside the taco stand and talk to the diving guests to convince them to try his family's famous tacos. While doing that, he would also talk to the guys and girls working at the dive shop and ask questions about the equipment.

After several years of chitchatting with the people working at the dive shop, the owner asked Carlos if he wanted to get his scuba diving certification. If he was interested in getting his license, the owner would eventually employ him as one of the local diving guides. Carlos jumped at the opportunity because although he loved working with his family, he didn't want to hustle people to buy tacos for the rest of his life.

After a few years of working at the dive store next to his parent's *taqueria,* the owner of the dive shop had a heart attack, and the diving operation shut down. At first, Carlos thought he would have to go back to selling tacos, but then he decided to go to Cozumel after he heard the other diving guides say they were going there to try to find work as guides. Carlos had never been out of Cancun except for taking the diving guests to Tulum to dive in the famous Mexican *cenotes*, which were big sinkholes in the jungle that were filled with water. So, after telling his parents his plans to go to Cozumel, he bought a one-way ferry ticket to the island known for its famous diving sites. Carlos said *Diving with Scuba Mar* was the first place he looked for work. After talking to the owner (the same guy that wouldn't bail out his own employee from jail), he got a job right away.

With a sigh, I thought how strange the whole situation was.

It didn't take me long to decide I was going to help my new friend and find out who really killed Drew. I opened up the door to the balcony and sat in one of the two lounge chairs. Resting back on the lounge chair, I breathed in the fresh salty air and thought about how I was going to help my friend.

Chapter Seventeen

I was jotting notes on the complimentary hotel notepad and pen when Julia came back from the lobby bar to find me sitting in a lounge chair on the balcony staring out at the sea.

"Hey Claire, what are you doing?"

I dropped my pen.

"Oh, hey! How was the bar?"

"It was okay. The girls found some cute guys they wanted to talk to, so I decided to come up and check on you. By the way, the cute guy from your scuba diving group showed up at the bar with his friend."

"You mean, Aiden?" I straightened up. Suddenly, I was more interested.

"Yeah, that's him. He was looking around for someone, maybe he was looking for you." Julia plopped down on her bed to take off her sandals.

"And?" I motioned with my hand for more details.

"And what? I thought you weren't interested in him." Julia said innocently, but I could see the twinkle in her eyes and knew that she was teasing.

"Okay, I admit I'm interested in him." I threw my hands up in defeat.

Julia gave me a "I knew it" look and added, "well, I don't know if he found who he was searching for, but Annisa made her way over to him."

"She what!" I jumped up from the chair again and walked over to Julia. "Did she start flirting with him?" I demanded placing my hands on my hips.

"I'm not sure, but they weren't talking for very long before Aiden and his friend left."

I stepped back in surprise. "Really? Aiden walked away from Annisa?"

"That's what I just said." Julia kicked off her flip flops and brought her legs onto the bed.

"I know. I just had to confirm it." My initial fear was replaced by giddiness thinking how shocked Annisa must have been when Aiden walked away.

I know I just met Aiden and had no reason to be possessive, but it felt wrong for Annisa to try to flirt with him.

"So, what were you thinking about when I walked in? You had a troubled look on your face." Julia said changing the topic. I guess she wasn't concerned by Annisa's behavior.

"Um.. I was just thinking about what happened to Carlos. I can't believe the police think he had anything to do with Drew's death."

Julia sighed when I gave my opinion about Drew's death. "Oh no. I've seen that look before. You're going to try to find out what happened to Drew aren't you?"

Julia's chastising expression told me she wasn't happy I was about to deviate from our weekend bachelorette plans. She was most likely thinking about the time when we were roommates at college when someone stole my mountain bike. I became obsessed about finding who took it, and even skipped classes to follow tips that were given to me by people who lived in the same dorm. If one person would say, "Claire, I think I saw your bike parked in the bike rack in front of the Union," I would stop whatever I was doing and head over to the area my bike was last seen. There were many misleads, but eventually I found my bike abandoned in the parking lot of an apartment complex near the campus. I never found out who stole my bike, but at least I got it back.

"I'm seriously thinking about delaying my flight back home for a few days."

"What do you think you can do?" Julia asked.

"I'm not sure, but I don't know if anyone is helping Carlos."

"What about the dive shop? Doesn't the owner have some responsibility to help one of his employees?" She was still skeptical of me being involved in finding out what happened to Drew. Julia probably thought I should leave things to the professionals.

"I would think so, but the dive shop owner said he fired Carlos after Drew complained about him. Well, at least I think it was Drew that complained about him."

"Oh man! Do you think that's why the police took Carlos? Getting fired because of someone's complaint seems like a motive to me." Despite the fact Julia didn't want me to get involved, she seemed interested in what happened to Carlos.

"Maybe, but what was the complaint? I bet Drew was the one to start the argument" I mulled over what might have happened.

"All the owner told me was someone complained that if he didn't fire Carlos, then he was going to write negative reviews about the diving company. The owner figured the easiest thing to do was to placate a troublesome guest rather than stick up for one of his best employees. It's not right Julia!" As I recounted the details of Carlos' firing, the angrier I got.

"So, you decided you're the one to help him." Julia seemed skeptical.

I paused by the weight of the words and the implications Julia was alluding to, but I nodded my head and smiled determinedly.

When Julia saw my lips drawn together a firm, thin line, she knew I was not going to leave Cozumel until I found who killed Drew and helped release Carlos. I could be stubborn.

"Okay Claire. I see you aren't going to let things go, but I hope you are able to find more information soon because I really don't want you to miss the wedding."

"I'll try my best, but if I don't, I'm sure Annisa would be happy to jump in my place as the maid of honor." Julia looked taken back at my answer. She paused for a few seconds, but eventually, she said, "Ha, ha!" Julia grabbed one of her pillows and threw it at me.

"Hey!" I batted it away before it hit my face.

Julia knew that I was joking, but she also knew that I was right. Annisa would love to jump in the spotlight and take over as the maid of honor.

Chapter Eighteen

I woke up to the the pitter patter of the rain against the window.

"Oh no!" I grabbed my phone to check if I had received any text messages.

"We are so sorry for any inconvenience, but this morning's dive is canceled. Please call our office to reschedule or for a refund," I read the text on my phone.

I bet the morning dive was canceled due to the rain and high winds. The rain itself wouldn't cancel the diving trip, but the strong winds would have made it impossible for the small scuba boats to head into the marine park. Looking out the window at the lashing rain, I was glad I wasn't going out on the choppy water. It was one of those days that made you just want to stay inside and read a cozy book while looking at the rain outside.

I looked over and saw Julia was still asleep in her bed, so I quietly got dressed in cutoff jean shorts and a t-shirt with the slogan, *mermaid hair, don't care.* I thought the slogan was fitting since I could never keep my hair tucked in a ponytail when I dove. After a few hours of diving and pulling my mask on and off my head, my hair resembled a matted bird's nest. I probably looked more like Medusa than a mermaid, but like the slogan said, *who cares?* Before I left the room, I brushed my teeth and ran a brush over my hair and went in search for some coffee.

The lobby was empty, but the bar was open.

"*Disculpe, ¿puedo tomar un café?*" I asked the bartender who was putting away clean glasses into a cabinet.

"*¡Claro!* Would you like cream and sugar?"

"*No, gracias.*"

The bartender set down the glass he was drying and went over to the espresso machine. I listened to the stream of coffee dripping into a dainty white porcelain cup. When the coffee stopped flowing into the cup, the bartender brought me my first coffee of the day. I stared at the small portion and grimaced. Being an American, I was used to drinking from a larger cup. I am going to need at least three cups of this I thought.

"*¡Gracias!* I was about to walk away, but I stopped after a few steps.

"*Disculpe, señor*. Do you have a pen and paper I can use?"

The bartender looked around, but he didn't see anything.

"I'm sorry, perhaps, you can ask the receptionist if they have paper and a pen."

"Sure, that's a good idea." I continued walking until I reached the front desk. Lupe was working again.

"Hi Lupe, do you remember me?" I asked thinking she probably wouldn't. There must be a least a few hundred guests that check in and out of the hotel on a daily basis, so I was surprised when she said, "yes, I remember. You asked me where you could find the hotel manager." She smiled. "Do you need to look for him again?"

I laughed. "Oh no, not today. I was wondering if you had some paper and something to write with that I could borrow."

Lupe reached under the desk and pulled out a few pages of hotel stationery and handed them to me. Then she reached for one of the pens that was sticking out of a glass vase. "You can keep this." She said as she handed me a pen that said *Cozumel Grand*.

"Great! *¡Gracias*!" I took my loot to one of the glass top tables and set them down. I pulled out and sat on one of the wicker chairs.

I tapped the pen against my lips as I concentrated.

"Okay. So, who were all the people that Drew may have offended?" I asked myself rhetorically, but then I realized the list of people would be incomplete because I only saw him talking to the other divers and some people from the bachelorette party. Who knew how many other people Drew had offended at the resort that I didn't witness. Rather than being discouraged by that thought, I wrote down a list of names of people who I did see talking to him.

Ryan, Aiden, Peyton, Margaret and Tom Tanaka, Carlos, Marcos, Emma, Annisa, and of course-

"Why are you writing my name on the piece of paper? Who are Ryan, Aiden, Pey-"

I heard Annisa's say the names just as I was about to write my own name. I looked up and saw her standing next to the table and looking over my shoulder at the piece of paper. As usual, she looked stunning. Annisa was wearing a white halter dress. And even this early in the morning, her hair and makeup were perfectly done.

"Hey, good morning!" I said as I tried to surreptitiously move my forearm over the names. "What are you doing up so early?"

Annisa rolled her eyes and gave me a look. "It's 8:00. It's not that early."

Wow-so in order for her to look like that, Annisa must have gotten up at least an hour ago. Mystified why a person would want to spend so much time looking good, I temporarily forgot Annisa's question.

"Why is my name on the paper?" she demanded. She didn't

seem mad, but she was definitely curious to what I was doing, and I debated whether I should confess my actions. Not having a good excuse, I decided to come clean. Maybe, Annisa could tell me if she saw Drew speaking to anyone else that I didn't already have on my list.

"I was making a list of all the people I saw talking to Drew," I admitted in embarrassment.

"Why?" Annisa's gaze was direct, and I had a hard time looking at her in the eyes. Annisa and Julia were so different that it was difficult to imagine they were friends.

"I wanted to make a note of everyone who had contact with Drew before he died."

"Do you think I had anything to do with his death?" Annisa asked incredulously. She was about to grill me, but Julia had arrived and sensed things were getting out of hand.

"Claire is trying to help her friend Carlos," Julia explained. "And, of course Claire doesn't think you had anything do with it." She said soothingly and gave me a look that said you better agree!

"Yeah, of course, I don't think you had anything to do with Drew's death. I'm just making a list." I replied as convincingly as I could.

Julia relaxed her shoulders at diffusing a tense situation, and said brightly, "I'm hungry, and I need some coffee. Let's get breakfast!" I wasn't ready to stop making my list, but Julia grabbed my hand and pulled me from my chair. I barely had time to grab the paper and pen before I was whisked away.

Chapter Nineteen

With one arm linked through mine and the other arm linked through Annisa's, Julia propelled us to one of the restaurants that served breakfast. Each day, one of the three resort restaurants rotated on offering breakfast. Today, the seafood restaurant opened its doors for the morning meal.

"I met this really cute guy at the bar last night," Annisa said just before we entered the restaurant.

I stopped in my tracks and looked at Julia. She looked back and gave a small shrug.

"Oh really? Who?" I tried to make my voice sound calm, but my insides were flipping around like someone was doing cartwheels.

"I think his name was Aiden, or maybe it was Adam. It was loud, so I couldn't hear well." Annisa said this breezily. To her, Aiden was another cute guy she met, and she didn't know that I knew him.

"Did you talk much?" I asked, trying act like I didn't care.

"Not really. I thought he was going to ask me if I wanted a drink, but he said he was looking for someone and had to go."

Annisa seemed befuddled that anyone wouldn't want to talk with her.

I felt relieved Aiden left so quickly after meeting Annisa. Although, I was surprised he didn't stay and talk with her. Most guys would have fallen over their feet trying to impress a pretty woman like Annisa Choi, and she knew it.

I looked at Julia, and she gave my arm a squeeze. She knew I was feeling insecure about Annisa meeting Aiden.

We walked into the seafood entrance and was greeted by a beautiful view of the sea.

"*¡Buenos días!*" The receptionist said walking towards us. "How many people will be dining this morning?"

"There will be six of us," Julia replied.

"*¡Excelente!* Please follow me. The three of us trailed behind the host as he made his way to the back of the restaurant. He sat us at a large table next to the window looking out the pool.

"Wow, this is a great view!" I remarked.

The view of the empty pool and the sea beyond calmed the flustered feeling I felt by being disrupted from my list and Annisa meeting Aiden. We sat down and ordered coffee while we waited for the other girls to arrive for breakfast.

"What do you guys want to do today?" Julia asked absent-mindedly as she picked up a menu to see what she wanted to eat.

While we were looking at the menu, the other girls appeared at the table looking a little groggy due to a lack of caffeine. I also noticed that, like me, they were dressed casually.

"It's too bad it's raining outside," Emma said as she plopped down on a chair next to me and looked wistfully out the window. "I wanted to go on a catamaran boat ride today."

Annisa dropped the menu and looked up at Emma with a horrified expression.

"That sounds terrible! The wind and rain would mess up my hair!" Annisa exclaimed. I knew Annisa was being honest when she said this, but Emma and I made eye contact and smothered our laughter.

I felt Julia kick me under the table, and I stopped laughing.

"It does sound awful right now. My head is pounding," Olivia said agreeing with Annisa. She had stayed out with Michelle last night talking to some guys at the bar, so she was looking a little rough.

"I need more coffee and water," Michelle moaned as she lunged for the pitcher of water.

Despite staying up late and being a little tipsy this morning, it seemed supremely unfair that Olivia and Michelle still looked cute in their yoga pants and oversized sweatshirts. If I had stayed up all night, I would probably look like something the cat dragged in the house. It was unfair.

I took a sip of coffee and looked around the restaurant. Spotting *señor Domínguez*, the owner of the dive shop, and Antonio, one of the other dive guides cut short my pity party. hey were by the pool talking, but Antonio looked upset. I wonder if *señor Dominguez* was giving him information about Carlos.

I wanted to go and find out what the men were talking about, but the waiter came to take our food order. By the time the waiter finished taking our breakfast choices, the men had disappeared from view. I wondered if they went to the scuba shop. I decided after I finished eating, I would make my way to the shop and find out if there was any news about Carlos.

"We never got around to figuring out what we wanted to do," Julia said and looked around the table when the waiter left.

"I vote to make it a spa day," Olivia said in a muted voice. She had ordered a Bloody Mary instead of food hoping it would cure her headache.

"I second a spa day," Michelle said and raised one hand over her head in emphasis. She looked better than Olivia and judging from the fact she also ordered an omelette, she was feeling better too.

"I guess I can go for a spa day," Emma said agreeably. As usual, Emma was game for anything.

"I don't know. I already did my hair and makeup. I don't want to mess it up." Annisa said and patted her coiffed hair.

"Why don't you get a manicure and pedicure?" Julia suggested. "In fact, why don't we all get mani-pedis?

"What about you Claire? Does this sound good to you?" Annisa asked, bringing the spotlight to me. "I know that you're watching your budget," she added innocently.

"It's fine. That sounds great!" I said ignoring Annisa's fake smile, but I dreaded the thought of being in a room with my hands and feet trapped. Other women would have loved to have a spa day, but I would rather be diving.

"It's settled. Let's swing by the concierge after breakfast and make an appointment," Julia said with a satisfied smile.

Our food arrived, and I ate without talking. I was too preoccupied thinking about what Antonio and the dive shop owner were talking about.

"Are you ready to go?" Annisa asked.

"Are you guys done?" I pushed back my chair and got up to see that Annisa was annoyed by my lack awareness.

"I swear Claire, you're so out of it sometimes!"

I knew she wanted to say something more, but Emma came up and put her arm around my shoulder. "This is going to be so much fun!" She squealed in excitement.

"Yay!" I said trying to echo her enthusiasm.

Emma gave me another shoulder hug and walked to the front of the group as we walked out of the restaurant.

"You don't seem enthused by a man-pedi," Julia said while walking along with me out the restaurant.

"No, that's not it. I was hoping to do something else today," I replied.

"Oh, that's right! Your dive got canceled this morning. I'm sorry."

"Yeah..," I responded letting Julia think that I wanted to go diving rather than trying to find out what *señor Domínguez* and Antonio were talking about.

"Cheer up Claire, having a self-care spa day won't be that bad, and we'll all get to spend more time together. Julia smiled as she said this and walked over to talk to Michelle and Olivia.

Spending more time with the other girls would be great, but spending additional time with Annisa was exactly what I didn't want to do. But I didn't want to spoil everyone's fun, and I had been MIA (missing in action) since we arrived in Cozumel, so I decided to be a good maid of honor and go along with the flow.

Chapter Twenty

Fortunately for me, Julia was unable to get a spa appointment for all of us together until later. This gave me some time to snoop around the dive shop. I gave Julia the excuse I was going to check on what dives were scheduled for tomorrow and headed out to the dive shop.

The shop's door was closed, but I saw Elena from the window.

"¡Hola!" I said as I opened the door and walked in.

"¡Hola Claire! Elena smiled when she saw me approach the counter. "I'm sorry the weather made us cancel the dives today. I know you are not staying on the island for very long."

"That's okay. It happens." I shrugged my shoulders indicating I understood these things happened sometimes.

"What can I do for you?"

"Oh, I saw *señor Domínguez* and Antonio talking by the pool, and I was wondering if they said anything about Carlos."

Elena's sunny disposition faded when I mentioned Carlos. "No, I haven't heard anything about Carlos."

"Is *señor Domínguez* or Antonio around?" Then, I heard some whimpering. I looked behind Elena at the room where they kept all the rental scuba diving gear. I couldn't see anyone, but there were noises coming from the room.

Elena saw where my attention was and turned around to see what I was looking at.

"What's that noise?"

Elena stopped moving, so she could hear what I was talking about. In the silence, both us could make out the scratching and what seemed to sound like whining.

"Oh, that's Luna," Elena whispered and looked around the room furtively.

"Who's Luna?" I asked quietly mirroring her volume.

"She's a dog that has been hanging around the dive shop. We don't know her real name, and I don't think she has a home. We have been giving her food and water the last few months, and she has been hanging around the shop. Actually, Carlos was the one taking care of her, and he even bought a little dog house to put in the back-room. We have to keep Luna out of sight because *señor Domínguez* doesn't like dogs. I think he is allergic to them, or that's what he said one time when another dog was wandering around the property."

"I'm taking care of Luna since the police have taken Carlos, but I think the dog really misses him." Elena explained and then she brightened up.

"Do you want to see her? She asked getting up from the stool she was sitting on.

"Oh, sure!" I was surprised by the turn of events, but I wouldn't give up the opportunity to see an adorable dog. I went behind the counter and followed Elena through the storage room door. Tucked behind some air tanks was a little dog house. I squatted down in front of the dog door and peeked in.

"Aww- how precious!" Inside was a little brown and white chihuahua. "Can I hold her?" I opened the dog door before Elena could say yes.

"Hi there sweetie!" I scooped up the little dog and brought

her close to my chest. Luna started licking my face and scratched my hand with her little paws.

"She doesn't like being locked up, but I have to keep her in the dog house while *señor Domínguez* is in the building, but when he leaves, I let her out," Elena said. This explained why Luna was so excited to be let out.

"Do you know where *señor Domínguez* is? I asked my original question before I was distracted by Luna's scratching and whimpering.

"No, I don't. He came into the shop this morning, but after we canceled the day's dives, he told me he was going to do errands the rest of the day. I was going to let Luna out after he left, but then you arrived."

"What about Antonio? Have you seen him?"

"No, I haven't seen Antonio. *Señor Domínguez* must have called all the dive guides to let them know they didn't have to come into work."

"Oh, really? I thought I saw Antonio talking with *señor Domínguez* this morning by the pool."

Elena shrugged. Apparently, I was the only one who saw Antonio. I was disappointed that neither men were available to talk to, but at least I got to meet Luna.

"What are you going to do with Luna?" I asked still holding the little dog. By now, Luna had calmed down and settled against my chest.

"I guess I'll keep taking care of her until Carlos gets out of jail." Elena said this convincingly, but judging from her expression, it was clear that she hadn't thought about what would happen to Luna.

"Do you think Carlos had anything to do with Drew's death?" I asked.

"No way!" Elena answered emphatically. I didn't know *señor* Drew very well, but he didn't seem like a nice person, and Carlos is the nicest guy. She shook her head to emphasize the point that Carlos couldn't be involved in Drew's death.

I looked at Luna to see that she had fallen asleep. Aww... she was so cute! I wanted to keep holding her, but I reached out to Elena to give her Luna. I was dismayed I hadn't found any information that would be helpful, but time had run out, and I had to get back for the mani-pedi session. *Woo-hoo*, I thought sarcastically.

I gave Luna a soft pat on the head and told Elena I would see her later.

With a wave, I left the shop and headed back to the resort lobby when I saw *señor Domínguez* talking to someone in a large black sedan. I was puzzled by his appearance because Elena said he left to go into town. Yet, he was in the dive shop parking lot.

I moved a little closer to see who he was talking to, but the tinted window wasn't open all the way, and *señor Domínguez's* tall frame obscured the view.

I wasn't going to interrupt the dive shop owner, so I continued to the lobby, but I was definitely intrigued by whoever was in the vehicle.

Chapter Twenty-One

The next morning, the girls gathered in the lobby to arrange their ride to the airport. It was there I broke the news I wouldn't be heading home with the rest of them. I didn't tell them I would be trying to find out how Drew died. Only Julia knew that. Instead, I told the girls that Carlos didn't have anyone to help him get out of jail, so I was going to stay and try to persuade the dive shop owner to bail him out. It was the least he could do for his former employee.

During our spa session yesterday, somehow the topic of Drew's death was brought up, and Julia told everyone Carlos was fired because one of the dive shop guests complained about him. They were outraged a guest could be such a jerk to get someone fired. Although they didn't know what the reason behind the firing was, they assumed that the cause couldn't be as bad as to get someone fired.

With the help of the concierge, the girls were able to get a van that served as a taxi to the airport.

"I wish you were coming back with us."

"Me too Jules!"

My best friend gave me a stern look. "Don't do anything foolish. Okay?"

"I promise," I replied trying to reassure her as best as I could. I just needed to figure out what to do.

Julia gave me one last hug and said goodbye before walking away to get in the waiting vehicle. Once everyone and their luggage was neatly packed in, the van drove around the circular driveway of the resort front area. I waved at the girls as the van came around again, and the girls enthusiastically waved back. Annisa looked a little too cheerful to see me standing there by myself while everyone else was heading back home. It did seem a little lonely to be standing there when everyone had left, but I told myself that it was my choice, and I needed to get started on finding out how to help Carlos.

However, the first thing I needed to do was to find another lodging place. When the girls checked out this morning, it also meant I had to vacate the resort as well because Julia was the one who paid for the room. Although I loved staying at the all-inclusive resort, the daily cost was out of my price range. I looked around the lobby to see if there was anyone who could recommend some place where I could stay that was inexpensive but safe. I scanned the room and saw guests dressed in various swimwear and some who looked like they were dressed to go on a jungle safari ride.

In addition to having beautiful diving sites, Cozumel also had Mayan ruins that the guest could experience. Visitations to these ruins were usually set up by the hotel staff with a tour company that charged more than if you went by yourself. But the tours came with an English-speaking guide that could give a better insight to what the visitors were supposed to look at. I remembered when I went on a tour of a Mayan ruin the last time I was in Mexico, and I had to admit that if it weren't for the guides, I wouldn't have known what I was looking at. Instead, I probably would have gone to the site, and remarked how cool everything was and then would want to leave twenty minutes later. With the help of the guide's knowledge, I learned so much more about the significance of the Mayan culture.

However, dressing like they were going to go on a safari was a bit much, which made me smile. Really, all one needed was a good pair of walking shoes, water, and mosquito repellent. In addition to inheriting my family's ability to gain and retain weight, I also inherited my mother's ability to attract every mosquito within sight. Julia used to joke she didn't need to wear mosquito repellent when I was around. It was aggravating how I seemed to be the only one that got bitten, but I joked it was because I was sweeter.

Behind an American couple dressed in matching scuba diving t-shirts that said *Cozumel*, I spotted Antonio. I waved my arm in the air to get his attention and called out, *"¡Hola, Antonio!"*

He turned around to see who was trying to get his attention, and when he spotted me, he smiled and shouted back, *"¡Hola, Claire!"*

Boy, this was good timing I thought.

I picked up my two suitcases and walked to where Antonio was standing.

I reached Antonio and greeted him again. *"¡Hola Antonio! ¿Cómo te va todo?*

"Muy bien, ¿y tú?" asked Antonio.

"Bien," I replied

"So, are you excited to go home today?" Antonio assumed I was leaving today because I mentioned it on the first day that I dove with the company.

"Well actually, I'm not going home. I decided to stay a few more days."

"Realamente?" asked Antonio surprised and a little confused. "I hope everything is okay."

"Everything is fine. I just wanted to stay a little longer in

Cozumel," I said, not giving him the real reason why I wasn't leaving. "But, since my friends have checked out of the hotel, I was wondering if you could recommend another place that is more... uh..."

"Less expensive," replied Antonio knowingly. I nodded with a sheepish grin. Even though there were a lot of people who had requested the same thing as me, I felt weird and embarrassed about asking for a place that was more affordable.

"A friend of mine who used to be a dive master owns a hostel that is close to the hotel." Antonio said and continued on to tell me more about the place. According to him, it was more like a house, but it had five separate rooms with its own bathrooms. It was located just a few blocks from the resort, and if I wanted to walk there to check it out, Antonio would call the owner.

"How much are the rooms per night?" I asked. I was mentally calculating how much I could afford for the extra few days that I was going to stay on the island.

"I think about 1,500 pesos per night, but you may be able to work with the owner to get a cheaper price," said Antonio.

"Wow, that's great," I said surprised by the cost. 1,500 Mexican pesos was equivalent to $78 US dollars. Buoyed by the good news, I asked Antonio to give me directions to the hostel that was named *La Casa Tranquila* and call to let the owner know I was on my way now.

"Ok, I will call Maria and let her know to expect you in about 10 minutes," said Antonio.

"*Excelente! Gracias amigo*. Oh, by the way, did you hear anything more about Carlos?

Antonio's eyes grew wide, and he said, "no, I'm sorry. I haven't. Why?"

"I was just wondering if you had more information about Carlos." I replied not mentioning that I saw him and *señor Domínguez* talking by the pool.

He looked at me puzzled that I would take such an interest in a diving guide I just met.

'Well, thanks for helping me find another place to stay," I said picking up the handles to my two suitcases. I wanted to get away before I said too much to Antonio.

I slung my travel purse over my shoulder and walked towards the street. I peeked over my shoulder and saw he was still looking at me strangely.

When I got to the sidewalk that paralleled the road, I was greeted by honking from approaching taxis. This short little burst of noise was similar to a request by the taxi driver letting me know that if I needed a ride, I only had to raise my hand, and the vehicle would stop when they got to me. I liked this method much better than in other countries, where the taxi drivers would stick their entire head out the window and yell at me like they did when I was in Indonesia. It was really nerve-wracking to walk down the streets and have a bunch of strange men yelling at you.

This was why whenever I planned a scuba diving trip, I made sure that my lodging and the scuba diving shop were located on the same grounds or a very, short walking distance. I didn't want to have to take a taxi unless it was to and from the airport. Even then, I tried to book a hotel that included transportation.

Just as Antonio described *La Casa Tranquila*, it was a small, but a neatly kept hostel.

The entrance was framed by palm trees, and there was a small wooden sign that read *"Bienvenida a La Casa Tranquila."* The building itself was placed further in from the street, but I could see that there were several wooden doors for the different rooms. As I walked towards the hostel, a tall woman appeared from inside the nearest door and walked towards me with an extended hand.

"Ah, you must be Claire!" she said with a firm but low voice. Actually, I found her voice to be very relaxing like those of yoga instructors. For a brief moment, I was distracted by wondering if Maria taught yoga but came back to reality when Maria asked me if I had any difficulty finding the hostel.

"No, I didn't have any problems finding the place," I answered. "Antonio gave me great directions, and it was a nice walk."

"Wonderful! So, Antonio said you are interested in renting a room for a few days, *Sí*?"

"*Sí*, that's correct."

"Would you like to see the rooms I have available?" Maria asked as she started to walk towards the house and motioned for me to follow her. "I currently have two rooms you can choose from. One is bigger than the other, but the smaller room has a better view of the sea. Come, and you can see for yourself."

Maria and I passed the first two doors until she reached the last door of the two-story stucco building that was painted a bright flamingo pink. Typical of the Spanish architecture of the early 19th century, the building had arched windows and mosaics textures on the walls. It created a romantic look. Adding to the vibe was a tall stone fountain in the middle of the courtyard that was spraying water upwards in a nice arc. The sound of the water hitting the pool where the fountain was located made the atmosphere quaint and relaxing.

"I love the décor of your place," I said to Maria.

"*Gracias.* When I bought this place seven years ago, the building was rundown, and the grounds were overgrown with weeds. It took two years of hard work to fix the plumbing and electrical wiring, but it was necessary to make this house comfortable for the guests. Without it, I couldn't have installed the air conditioning units for each room or update the showers to get a steady stream of water. These days, the tourists want all the comforts of a modern hotel even in a small boutique hostel such as this one," explained Maria. "I even have free Wi-Fi for the guests."

"Wow, that's great!" I exclaimed. Although free internet was common in most places that people stayed at in Cozumel, some places charged the guests for using the Wi-Fi. But it seemed like I had lucked out in this department as well.

I nodded in appreciation while I continued to look around me. To my surprise, I noticed there was a large colorful bird that looked like a parrot sitting on one of the branches in one of the trees in the courtyard. "Is that a parrot?" I asked in amazement.

"Why yes, that's Fernando," laughed Maria. He was my son's parrot, and we had him for over ten years. When my son Miguel helped me get this place ready for business, he would bring Fernando in his cage because he worked long days with me. I couldn't afford contractors, and Miguel is my oldest son, who is also an engineer living in Cancun. When I told him that I bought a place to fix up as a hostel, he agreed to come stay with me over the weekends for several months to help me get ready. So, each time Miguel came to Cozumel, he would bring Fernando with him.

At first, Miguel kept the bird in a cage, but one day he wanted to see if Fernando would prefer being in the trees in the courtyard rather than in a cage all day. I asked him if he was afraid that Fernando would fly away, but Miguel just shrugged. He figured if Fernando really wanted to be free, letting him go in Cozumel was better than in Cancun."

I agreed that was true especially since there was so much of Cozumel that was forested. When most people think of Cozumel, they think about the beaches. However, most people do not realize that only a small portion of the island is developed, and it is mostly on the western side of the island.

Maria continued to tell me the story, "so, when Miguel opened the cage door, Fernando hesitantly stepped through the opening and flew towards the sky. At first, we thought he was going to fly away from the hostel, but within a few hours, he came back and landed on a branch where you see him now.

When Miguel came here for the last time, he decided to leave Fernando here for good to keep me company. Even though Fernando flies off the property from time to time, he always comes back to the same branch you see him on now."

"Wow," I said. "That's an amazing story. In any case, Fernando certainly makes your place livelier and unique from others."

Maria smiled and nodded in agreement.

"Well, here we are," said Maria. She stood in front of a door that had the number three on it. She took out an old-fashioned iron key and stuck it into the lock. She turned the mosaic glass knob and opened the heavy wooden door and stepped aside so I could enter first.

The initial thought I had was that it was bigger than it looked from the outside and airier. The room had high ceilings even though it was on the ground floor. I stepped into the room, which was covered in square brown tiles. Immediately to the left of the front door was the bathroom. It was spacious with a walk-in shower and a decent sized vanity area with a sink. I noticed there were several soaps and lotions from what looked like a local vendor on a rattan cosmetic organizer which also held some personal toiletries. Opposite the bathroom door was a closet with a bar across that held some hangers. I also spotted a newer looking safe on top of the shelf above the wooden bar. When I saw this, I felt better about leaving my stuff behind. Not that I had a lot of valuables, but I didn't want my passport or driver's license stolen, and I planned on locking up my dive computer and camera whenever I was not in the room.

Against one of the walls was a queen-sized bed with an intricate wooden headboard. The bedding quilt had a beautiful and colorful Mayan design with several fluffy white pillows. On the opposite wall was a dresser which held a medium size flatscreen smart TV. Next to the dresser was a small desk and chair. On the other side of the dresser was a mini refrigerator with two glasses and an ice bucket on top of it. At the end of the room was a set of French doors that opened to a small patio area. The patio was furnished with a small round wrought iron table with two matching chairs on either side. It would be perfect for drinking coffee in the morning or drinking a glass of margarita in the evening. It wasn't a large area, but it looked peacefully out to a sandy path that led to the beach.

"This is the larger of the two rooms," said Maria. "What do you think?"

"It's lovely," I replied. And it was. I could see myself relaxing outside with a cup of coffee in the morning.

"Well, before you agree to this room, why don't we take a look at the other room," said Maria before I could ask how much it cost to stay here for three nights. We walked out of room three and went to the staircase that was located close to the room's front door. We climbed up the stairs to the second floor and stopped directly above the previous room. This room was labelled number five on the outside of the heavy door. Similar to the last time, Maria took another clunky metal key from her pocket.

"How do you keep track of all the keys. They look identical," I asked trying to get a better look at the keys.

Maria laughed and said, "Yes, they do look alike, don't they? But, see here at the end of each key, the metal is flattened, and a number is engraved on each one." I bent down and looked closely at the key Maria was holding out for me and saw that it did indeed have a small number etched on it. However, it was really small, and in the dark, I doubted I could read the numbers.

Maria must have read my mind, and said, "in addition to the number, the end of each key is shaped differently." She pointed to the end of key number five, and I saw the end was shaped as a clover leaf, and when Maria held out the key for number three, I saw the end was shaped in an oval. "With only five rooms to worry about, it is simple to keep track of the keys by their shape."

"Ah," I said. "That makes sense. Although... how do you keep someone from copying the keys?"

"Well, there aren't many iron keys these days or people who know how to make them on the island, but if you are worried about losing your key while you are diving or going into town, you can always leave it with me, and I will put it in the safe at the front desk," explained Maria.

"Also, if you are worried about security, there is a wrought iron fence that surrounds this property. When you came in, the gate was open, but we shut the gate at dusk every day. The only way that you can go through is if you have a pass code, and we change the pass code daily. There is also a gate when you go a little way towards the back of the property, so you can come back directly to your room if you go to the beach, but that gate is always closed and locked, but you can open it with the same pass code as the front gate. Finally, we have security cameras throughout the grounds that are tied to an alarm system that is connected to a local security company.

"That's great!" I was impressed by all the security measures Maria had taken to keep her guests safe.

Maria turned the knob and opened the door to let me enter. I was met with a flood of light due to the large window that let in the morning sunlight. I went over to the window and looked out to see a beautiful view of the Caribbean Sea. Even though I couldn't go out of the room to a balcony, there was a large comfy recliner placed next to the window with a small end table that I could see myself sitting there with my notes about the investigation. I looked around the room to find it had similar furnishings as the room downstairs.

"What do you think?" asked Maria. "The room is comparable in size as the other room, but the room downstairs also has a patio you can walk out into, so I market it as a "larger room.""

"This room is perfect! I love the view," I said. "How much does this room cost to stay for three nights?'

"As Antonio told you, the rooms are 1,500 Mexican pesos, so it would come out to 4,500 pesos. However, I will let you stay for 4,000 pesos if that is agreeable to you," Maria replied.

I smiled broadly and said, "you got a deal!"

"Also, if you go down the stairs and head back toward the front of the property, the first door of the hostel is the room I use as the guest lobby. Inside there are a few tables and chairs where guests can relax and talk to other guests. Every morning, I lay out some coffee, juice, fresh fruit, and some pastries if you want to eat breakfast. Also, in the afternoons, I put out some more pastries you can eat with coffee or tea."

I looked at Maria in disbelief at all the personal touches she did for her guests. The next time I saw Antonio, I was going to tell him that he outdid himself with his recommendation.

Maria handed me the key to room number five and then left me to unpack my suitcase. After the door closed behind Maria, I reclined back on the queen-sized bed. "Ah, this is heaven!" I sighed. I laid down on the bed for a few minutes to think about what I needed to do next. It was still early in the morning. My watch said 10:00am. I didn't have any other leads, so I decided to walk back to the resort. Maybe there was someone at the dive shop I could talk to.

Chapter Twenty-Two

When I returned to the resort pier, I was expecting it to be busy, but the diving crew had already left with the boats for the morning. As a result, the shop was empty except for Elena.

"*¡Hola* Claire*!* Are you here for another day's dive? I thought you were leaving this morning." She lifted her eyebrows when she saw me walk in.

"*¡Hola Elena!* You're right. I was supposed to leave today, but I decided to stay a few extra days." I didn't add on I was staying to find out what happened to Drew and see if Carlos had anything to do with his death. I also wanted to make sure I didn't provide any information that could be passed accidentally to the real killer.

"How are you doing," I asked. Even though Elena looked like she was doing okay, I wanted to check since she was the one who found Drew's body.

"I'm okay," said Elena. "The whole situation seems unreal to me. I know many people didn't like *señor* Drew, but he was nice to me most of the time."

Probably because you are a pretty, young woman, I thought.

I winced- appalled at my train of thought, and I pushed that sexist thought from my head and asked another question.

"Is anyone else here other than you?" I inquired as I surveyed the shop.

"Other than *señor Domínguez*, the owner, everyone else is on the boats. We had a lot of people signed up to dive today. I think it's because it's getting to the end of your American winter holiday, and everyone wants to get in one last dive. After today, we have half as many divers as we did the last few days." Elena shook her head in wonder.

In the scuba diving industry, it was very much a feast or famine situation where in the high season, typically May through October, there are a ton of tourists that come to Cozumel, and many of them choose to dive for a day or two. There's also a mad rush during the last two weeks of December and the first week of January to coincide with the U.S. winter break. However, the unpredictable high winds during the winter make scuba diving riskier because the strong winds could force the ports to close.

Although people can still enjoy the beach and perhaps do a shore dive in a secluded area such as Tikila Beach, divers cannot access the Marine Park. Come to think of it, this was probably why Maria gave me a discounted price on the lodging. She wanted to make sure the price was attractive to me since the winter tourist season was winding down.

"Do you think I can talk to *señor Domínguez*?"

Elena was puzzled why I wanted to talk to the dive owner, but she said, "Sure. Just go up the stairs to his office."

"*Gracias,*" I replied as I started to walk up the staircase to the owner's office. At the top of the narrow staircase, I saw the office door was shut, so I raised my hand to knock on the door. My closed fist stopped in mid-air when I heard his voice say, "Yes, unfortunately, Carlos is still in the hands of the Mexican police. For some reason, they think he had something to do with one of our guests who died. Mmm.. hm. I really felt bad about letting Carlos go especially since I found out his parents died during the Covid pandemic, but I had no choice. The guest threatened to leave a bad review about my dive shop if I didn't comply," I heard the owner's muted voice say to whoever he was talking to.

I was about to knock on the door again when it opened with a whoosh. I stood in front of *señor Domínguez* still holding the cellphone next to his ear.

"*¡Dios mío!,*" said the startled man. He clutched his chest with his free hand.

"I'm so sorry to surprise you, *señor.* I was going to knock on your door, but you opened it before I could knock. I hope I'm not interrupting. *Señor Domínguez* held up one finger to indicate he wanted me to wait for a response, and he mumbled, "I have a customer here, so I have to go, but I will call you later."

The dive shop owner snapped his flip phone together with one hand and put it in his pocket.

"*Hola*, you are the *señorita* that asked about Carlos yesterday. *Sí?*"

"*Sí, señor.*" He looked like he was in a hurry, so I hastily asked my question. "I was wondering if you had any news regarding Carlos." I didn't want to mention I overheard *señor Dominguez's* conversation behind the closed door.

"Unfortunately, the police are still detaining Carlos at the precinct downtown." *Señor Domínguez* tried to move to the edge of the staircase, but I moved in front of him blocking his descent.

"Do you know when they are going to release Carlos?" I pressed.

"*No se,*" he said as he shook his head back and forth. He looked sad and thoughtful for a moment, but then remembered I was standing in front of him. He gave a quick shake of his head and blinked several times.

"If you are staying a little longer on the island, would you like to go on another dive?" *Señor Domínguez* asked.

Unprepared by the change of direction in the conversation, I stood rooted to the ground with my mouth slightly agape. I thought about his question for a few seconds because I hadn't planned on diving again. When I changed my plans to leave for The San Francisco Airport this morning along with the other girls, I didn't think of anything but trying to help Carlos get out of jail. Now that *señor Domínguez* mentioned diving, I thought I could do another day's worth diving. Perhaps if I went out with the crew, I might overhear additional information that could help release Carlos.

"I wasn't planning on going diving again, but I'm here in Cozumel for another few days, so I might as well add another day of diving," I finally answered *señor Domínguez.*

The thought of another day's worth of a paying customer using his dive shop services made the owner smile, and he said, "if you want to do another day of diving, you can sign up to do a two-tank dive tomorrow. Today, we had an extremely large group of divers, but tomorrow should be less crowded. In fact, I will give you a ten percent discount because you have previously dived with us before.

The mention of a discounted dive spurred me to blurt out, "that's great! *Gracias.* I will sign up with Elena."

"Estupendious," said the dive shop owner, and he gestured for me to walk down the stairs to the reception desk with him. When we approached the desk, he said, *"Elena, la señorita quiere ir al buceo manana."*

"Bueno, señor," replied Elena. She reached underneath the desk to grab a consent form for me to sign. "I won't go over the details again, but I need you to sign and date here, and pay 1,500 pesos.

Before I could mention I just received a discount, *señor Domínguez* said, "Elena, please give this nice young lady a ten percent discount because she's a great friend to the shop." With that, the owner winked at me and left the shop whistling.

He seemed to be in a better mood.

After signing and paying the dive fee, I glanced at the whiteboard that had all the week's dives, the guest list, and the dive guides that were planning to go on each trip. Many scuba diving operations let their guests choose what dive sites they wanted to go on, but this dive shop was one of the larger operations on the island because it was associated with a large resort hotel. Therefore, each day, the dive company listed the prescribed sites they would visit. For tomorrow's dive, I saw the two dives which most divers refer to as two tank dives were first to Palancar Horseshoe and then to Delilah.

I was excited about diving through the numerous arches of the Palancar reefs, and I smiled in anticipation. I also read Ryan, Aiden, Peyton, and the Tanakas were also going to be diving tomorrow. At the thought of seeing Aiden again, my heart fluttered. I didn't know if it was from dread or happiness. The last time I spoke to him was right after he gave me his California number, but then Elena's scream brought us all to the pier to find Drew's body. This also brought me back to the memory of the two detectives who interviewed Ryan, Aiden and Peyton about Drew's death. I hoped by now, the police had more leads that didn't involve Carlos.

Since there was no one else around, I decided to take a taxi downtown to see if the police would let me talk to Carlos. Perhaps he knew something that might help me find out how Drew really died. I walked to the front of the resort to flag one of the many taxis that were clustered around the entrance.

As I was about to get into a taxi, I saw the dive shop owner speak with someone inside a dark sedan. I didn't know if it was the same car as last time, but I found this suspicious.

"*Señorita*, are you getting in?"

The cab driver's voice jolted me.

"Uh-yes, I am. I pinched my lips as I shot another glance to where *señor Domínguez* was, but he was gone.

Frustrated I said, "could you please take me to the police station?"

The driver nodded and pulled into traffic. I leaned back against the seat and thought about who had a reason to harm Drew.

Chapter Twenty-Three

"We are here *señorita*," The driver said turning around to look at me.

"*Gracias señor!*" The trip from the resort to police station cost 300 Mexican pesos which was equivalent to about three US dollars. Even though the fare wasn't much, I had to watch my expenses. These extra days on the island weren't planned, and I currently wasn't earning any income. The money I had been using for the trip was saved during my last teaching job, and I had only budgeted for three days instead of six. Determined to save a few bucks, I decided to walk back to the hostel when I was done at the police station. The trip back should be shorter because the hostel was closer to downtown by a few blocks

I strolled to the entrance of the police station and opened the door. A blast of cool air from the air-conditioned building greeted me, and I walked toward the desk where a uniformed officer was sitting at a desk.

"*Discuple, señor?*" I said.

The uniformed officer looked up at me, and answered "*Si, señorita.* May I help you?"

"Yes, I am looking for my friend Carlos Santiago. He worked for Scuba Mar. Detectives Martinez and Rojas brought him into the station for questioning," I added.

"*Un momento*. Wait here please," said the officer as he got up from his desk. I didn't know where he was going until he walked out of a room with Detective Martinez, who was the tall female detective that questioned Aiden, Ryan, and Peyton at the resort, followed him out. She stopped in front of me with her arms crossed.

"*Sí, señorita?* May I help you? I understand you are inquiring about your friend Carlos?" Detective Martinez said in a clipped tone.

"Yes, I was wondering if you could tell me if you are going to release him soon." I tried to be as polite as possible.

"Unfortunately, we need to keep him for a little longer. Do you have any information that might help your friend?" asked Detective Martinez. She looked at me suspiciously as though I knew something. Then the detective's eyes grew wide as she recognized me. "Weren't you a diver that was on the same scuba diving company as the man that died at *Cozumel Grand*?"

"Yes, I was on the same boat as Drew," I admitted hoping she wouldn't think I had anything to do with his death.

The detective was silent for a moment, and I could only speculate what she was thinking, but I bet my money the detective was wondering why she didn't interview me along with the other people from the boat.

After several awkward seconds of Detective Martinez staring at me, she said, "*señorita*, please follow me to my office. I have some questions to ask you." Without waiting to see if I would follow her, she turned and walked to her office as she directed the officer to page Detective Rojas to her office.

"*¡Sí!*" The officer said and reached for the phone.

When we got to her office, Detective Martinez motioned for

me to sit in one of the chairs that was positioned in front of her desk.

"Would you like some coffee?" The detective asked as I lowered myself in a chair.

"Some coffee with sugar and cream would be excellent, thank you!" I said grateful for some caffeine. I drank coffee in the morning with the girls at breakfast, but now, the caffeine level was low, and I was starting to get a low-grade headache that usually came with a lack of caffeine.

Detective Martinez went to a small table behind me where there was a full pot of coffee with two small canisters that I assumed were filled with powered cream and sugar. The detective grabbed a Styrofoam cup and took a plastic spoon and scooped some cream and sugar into the cup without asking me how much I wanted. Then she poured the coffee into the cup and stirred it altogether with the plastic spoon. She handed me the cup of coffee and went to sit behind her desk.

"*Gracias,*" I said and took a sip. I tried hard not to make a face. Although the coffee was nice and hot, the detective put too much sugar into the coffee which caused it to taste like liquid sugar. With a shudder, I gulped the syrupy liquid that was already in my mouth down and decided to just hold the cup in my hands. We sat quietly for a few minutes before detective Rojas entered the room.

"*Buenos dias*, I'm Detective Rojas," he said to me and reached his hand forward to shake my hand.

"*Buenos dias,* I'm Claire O'Keefe."

He shook my hand firmly and then sat down on the other chair that was in front of Detective Martinez's desk.

From his brisk movements, I could tell he meant business like this his partner.

"So, what are we talking about?" he asked detective Martinez.

"This young lady, Claire, was on the same boat as the victim from *Cozumel Grand*. However, she was not interviewed," replied Detective Martinez. The detectives' eyes met with this statement, and it appeared as though there was a mutual agreement between them not to place blame on each other as to why I was not questioned along with the other guests."

"Ah-hem!" Detectives Rojas cleared his throat. "I see. So, Ms. O'Keefe, can you tell us how well you knew the victim?" He asked looking back at me.

I snuck a glance at Detective Martinez before I answered Detective Rojas. Both officers were looking at me intently hoping I could tell them something that would help them in their investigation.

"I didn't know Drew well," I replied. "We were on the same dives the last two days."

"What was your impression of the victim?" asked Detective Martinez.

"To be honest, I really didn't like him," I responded. I saw both detectives look at each other again. They knew from interviewing Ryan, Aiden, and Peyton's responses I shared the same sentiment.

"Why didn't you like him? Did he do or say anything in particular?" asked Detective Rojas. He brought out a small notepad and pen from inside his jacket to take notes.

I sighed as I thought back to a specific moment I could relay to the detectives, and I recalled a memory from one of the boat rides. "Yes, there was one time when Drew made a comment about my weight while I was trying to get off my wetsuit. He was being unkind, but I just ignored him," I said.

"What did he say?" Detective Rojas pressed me for a clearer answer.

I was embarrassed to say it, but I managed to squeak out, "well, he basically said that I was fat."

Detective Martinez's eyes bulged, and she cocked her head to one side when she heard the comment, but she didn't respond to

CINDY QUAYLE

my statement. The detective might have disapproved of Drew's comment, but she was a professional, and she seemed intent on being neutral.

"Did you see or hear him say anything that was unkind to anyone else?" asked Detective Martinez.

"No, I'm sorry. When Drew was around, I tried to find someplace else to be," I tugged on my ear in embarrassment. "I'm afraid he had that reaction from a lot of people that were on the boat. Again, the detectives made eye-contact and nodded.

"Is there anything else that you would like to tell us?" asked Detective Rojas.

"No, I can't think of anything. I'm here to check up on my friend Carlos. Can you tell me why you have him in custody, and can I talk to him?" I asked.

"I'm sorry, we can't let you talk to your friend unless you are his attorney, " replied Detective Rojas.

"That's disappointing." I said to the detectives. I stared at Detective Martinez hoping to think of another reason to see Carlos, but my mind went blank.

In desperation, I wondered what Annisa Choi would have done in my shoes. Annisa would have smiled coquettishly and batted her eyelashes at the detectives to change their minds.

Yikes, I can't do that. I would look foolish, and I snorted as I suppressed an involuntary laugh.

The detectives looked at me.

Finally I asked, "could you please tell Carlos his friend Claire from the diving group stopped by today?"

"Of course. If there is anything else you can remember, anything at all, please do not hesitate to contact me," said Detective Martinez as she handed me her business card. The detective stood up from behind her desk signaling the interview was over. She walked to the door and opened it. Then she motioned for me to go out and said, "I'll walk you to the front."

I got up and said goodbye to Detective Rojas and followed

Detective Martinez back to the reception area. The detective walked quickly with purposeful steps as though she had a million things to do and the last thing that she wanted was to escort me back to the lobby. We reached the area where the uniformed police officer was, and she said to me, "thank you for stopping by today, and I will let your friend know you asked about him."

"Thank you, and please tell Carlos if he needs anything to let me know," I said, but the detective had already turned away and was walking back to her office.

Well, that was a bust I thought as I walked out of the air-conditioned police building into the hot and humid air. I didn't learn why the police were detaining Carlos, and I wasn't able to speak with him either. With no other ideas, I walked back to the hostel.

Chapter Twenty-Four

After a forty-five minute walk, I turned the key to my room. I found the big comfy recliner and flopped into it and thought about how much quicker it took to get to downtown compared to walking back to the hostel. But I needed to save as much as I could so even though I was drenched in sweat, I congratulated myself on saving a couple dollars that I may have to use in the future.

With a sigh, I looked out at the beautiful, tranquil blue-green waters. The trip to the police station didn't yield much information, but at least I was able to convey a message to Carlos. I wondered what else I could do.

Although I didn't mean to, I ended up taking a nap in the recliner. I woke up to the sound of people around *La Casa Tranquila*. I blinked twice and tried to orientate my mind to the surroundings. The afternoon sunlight was pouring into my room making it bright and airy. I put my hands over my head and stretched as I launched myself out of the chair.

I became aware I missed lunch when my stomach growled unladylike. I decided the next step would be to find someplace to eat a late lunch or early dinner depending on what time it was.

The large numbers on my watch illuminated 3:40pm. I recalled Maria said she put out some pastries, coffee, and tea in the afternoon for her guests in the lobby, so I walked over there to see if I could find someone who could recommend someplace close by for a meal.

The door to the reception room was open, and I saw Maria talking to another guest. The guest was a woman that looked older than Maria, probably in her mid-fifties. In addition to the woman Maria was conversing with, there was a couple that was sitting at one of the small square coffee tables. Like the woman Maria was talking to, the couple looked older than the host.

Maria spotted me and waved me over to where she and the other lady were standing.

"*Buenos tardes* Claire," said Maria. Did you have a nice morning?"

"*¡Sí!*" I replied.

"Why don't you get some pastries and something to drink? I have some water infused with fruit if you don't want coffee or tea," said Maria.

"I'll take both," I was parched, and I hadn't had anything to drink since the syrupy coffee Detective Martinez made for me. I went to the side table where there were a few colored glasses and poured myself some water that had frozen fruit ice cubes floating in it. I took a drink and smiled at how refreshing the liquid was.

"Claire, I would like to introduce you to my friend, Lonnie, who is also a guest. She is staying in room two which is next to this room."

I reached over to shake Lonnie's hand. "Hello, nice to meet you."

Maria gestured to the couple sitting at the coffee table and said, "over there is Jack and Terry, and they are also guests at *La Casa Tranquila*." I looked over and instead of going over to the couple to shake their hands, I just waved hello. Jack and Terry looked at me and smiled and waved back.

It turned out that all the guests staying at *La Casa Tranquila* were scuba divers. In fact, all of them had known Maria for a long time when she first met them during her time as a diving guide with a local scuba diving operation. Jack and Terry were frequent visitors to Cozumel. They tried to come to the island every six months after retiring from their jobs in Arizona. Both Jack and Terry were former schoolteachers, and they were thrilled to meet another teacher. On the other hand, Lonnie was still working as a nurse in Massachusetts, so she could only get to Cozumel every other year because she had two grown children living in Maryland and Virginia that she wanted to spend time with.

After finishing up my fruit infused water, I went back to the sideboard and grabbed a colorful plate and filled it with pastries and poured myself a cup of coffee. I put a little cream in my coffee and omitted the sugar. In the mornings, I liked to drink my coffee black to wake me up. Whether the coffee tasted good or not was secondary to the much-needed caffeine. However, in the afternoon, I indulged myself by adding a little creamer to cut the bitterness. I brought my food and drink back to where Maria and Lonnie were standing.

"Lonnie, did you dive today?" I inquired.

"Yes, I did," replied Lonnie.

"Who did you dive with?" *Wow!* I bit into the bread and tasted the buttery softness.

"I dove with Scuba Mar," said Lonnie. "Normally, I don't like to dive with a company associated with resort hotels, but they were offering a discount if you paid for the dives online. Since today is my last day to dive, I figured I might as well take advantage of the great deal."

"Scuba Mar," I echoed. "That's the company I dove with too. I had stayed at the resort the last few days because I was there with some friends to celebrate my best friend's bachelorette party. I'm also diving with them again tomorrow."

"Oh, are your friends scuba divers as well?" asked Lonnie.

"Oh no," I laughed. "My best friend Julia got her open-water certification with me when we were sophomores in college, but she didn't like it, so she never dove after that. And the rest of the girls in the bachelorette party would rather stay on the surface of the water than below the waves.

"That's a shame," lamented Lonnie. "Your friends don't know what they're missing. I find it so peaceful and relaxing when I'm underwater. I would stay there all day if I didn't run out of air." Maria and I nodded in agreement because we knew how she felt.

"Where did the boat take you guys today?"

"Today, we went to Columbia and San Francisco." Even though Lonnie didn't add the word reefs, I knew she wasn't referring to the country or city but the dive sites. "It was a great day to dive, except when we were surfaced, all anyone could talk about was this guy Drew that was supposedly murdered by one of the crew members from Scuba Mar.

Based on the way the guests and the crew were talking, the man that was killed was not liked by anyone, and the person who the police think committed the crime was a really nice guy that couldn't have possibly killed the man. According to the lead dive master, the suspect was fired by the company right before the victim was killed, so it doesn't look good for the crew member." Lonnie shook her head at the information she heard during her morning dive.

When I heard this tidbit, I was more determined than ever to find out what was really going on. I hoped I was going to be on the same boat as Ryan, Aiden, and Peyton tomorrow, so I could ask them if they heard anything else from the time that the police interviewed them.

I visited with Lonnie and Maria until I finished off my pastries and the cup of coffee. I eyed the cheese danish on the side board wishing I could have another one, but I knew I should probably eat dinner.

"Do you know a good restaurant around here I can go for dinner?" I asked Maria and Lonnie.

Lonnie's eyes lit up. "There is a small family-owned restaurant that serves the best freshly caught seafood. The restaurant is difficult to find from the street, but if you go out the back gate and walk along the beach path, the restaurant is about a short fifteen-minute walk. There isn't a sign indicating the building is a restaurant, but it's painted a bright red, and it is next to a convenience store called the *La Bodega*. Also, the restaurant owners have set out several metal tables and chairs in different pastel colors."

I tilted my head to the side with a befuddled look on my face as I tried to imagine the décor Lonnie had just described.

"I know," she laughed. "The color scheme of the place is a little off, but trust me, the food is well worth it!"

I agreed to try the restaurant and with a wave goodbye to Maria and the guests, I walked out of the reception room back toward the rear of the property. I eventually found the back fence partly hidden by overgrown vines and used the key code to let myself out to the path going toward the beach. I made sure the gate was closed tightly behind me before I walked away.

Chapter Twenty-Five

I walked along the beach path and enjoyed the warm salty breeze. People were sunning themselves on the sand, but it didn't seem crowded. There was a large iguana lounging under a small bush, and I would have completely missed it if it hadn't been for a group of tourists, pointing at the poor lizard and taking pictures of it. The reptile seemed to have had enough of the humans' antics and darted completely under the bush.

The walk to the restaurant was short as Lonnie promised, and as she said, the restaurant was hard to miss because of its bright red color. I veered off the beach path and walked to a podium where a young lady was sitting. Even though the beach entrance was not the front of the business, the owners, figuring most people would find the restaurant from the beach side, put someone back there to greet guests.

The young lady smiled and said, "*bienvenidos*! Would you like a table?"

"*¡Sí!,*" I replied.

"How many people are in your party?" asked the hostess.

"Just me."

The hostess nodded and smiled and led me to the corner where there was a small table with two chairs. The hostess put down a set of cutleries wrapped in a cloth napkin, and as she walked away, she picked up the other chair. "This way, you won't be bothered." She winked before she added, "I can leave the chair if you would like."

"No, that's okay. You can take the chair." I smiled at her thoughtfulness. Apparently, the hostess was experienced in solo travelers who did not want to be hit on by strange men or women.

The waiter arrived with a glass of water just as the hostess was leaving. *"Hola amiga, bienvendios.* Here is a menu for you to look at. My name is Juan, and I will be your waiter tonight. I will give you a few minutes to look at the menu, and in the meantime, is there anything else you would like to drink?"

Although I knew I should save as much money as I could, I ordered a *mojito*. I rationalized I saved some money on my walk home from the police precinct instead of taking a cab. Therefore, I could indulge in just one cocktail.

"Excellent choice," Juan said and walked to the bar.

Looking at the one-page laminated plastic menu, I read the limited food selection. In the appetizer section, there were chips with *salsa, queso, or guacamole,* and for the main entrees, there were various types of tacos.

I scanned the menu to see something that caught my eye. "Lionfish tacos!"

At that moment, Juan came back with my *mojito.*

"Juan, am I reading this correctly? Does this item really say lionfish?" I asked thinking that it might be a typo.

Juan nodded his head, and said, *"Si,* that is correct. Lionfish tacos are our house specialty. They are caught everyday by the owner's daughter."

"Really?" I said incredulously.

"*Sí, La señorita* that brought you to this table is the owner's daughter. She is a skilled scuba diver, and almost every day she goes out and hunts for lionfish to help keep the predatory animal's population down while providing the restaurant with seafood," Juan explained.

I knew many divers went on lionfish hunting expeditions. The lionfish was an interesting species, and they were fun to look at underwater, but they were very poisonous. However, what made them especially dangerous was the fact they were not native to the waters of Cozumel, and they were rapidly expanding their population because the other fish could not eat them. It usually took a diver with a spear gun to take out the invasive fish. But I didn't know you could eat them once you caught them.

"That's so awesome!" Intrigued by what Juan had told me and in the spirit of being adventurous, I decided to try the lionfish taco.

It turned out that lionfish meat tasted like any other grilled fish, and the tacos were delicious. The flaky white meat was tender and charred to perfection.

Feeling stuffed and satisfied, I waved at Juan to get his attention.

"How was everything?" Juan asked when he reached the table.

"Oh, my goodness, it was excellent! I feel so full right now." I said and patted my belly.

"Is there anything else that I can get you?"

"No that's it. Just the bill please."

Juan left to retrieve the bill, but he came back shortly with a black tray with a piece of paper clipped to it.

"I'm glad you enjoyed your meal, and I hope you come again," he said as he set the small tray on the table.

I was excited when I picked up the bill and saw the entire

meal along with my drink came out to 110 Mexican pesos, which was about six dollars. What a great deal! I was grateful for Lonnie's suggestion, and I decided I would come back here tomorrow for dinner to try another restaurant specialty.

I paid the bill and said goodbye to Juan and Roberta, the hostess, and I walked back to the beach path. When I first got to the restaurant, I didn't pay much attention to my surroundings because I was starving. However, now that I was no longer hungry, I was able to focus on where I was. I realized I was located just beyond the resort I stayed at for the bachelorette party.

I looked around and noticed there were a few other local restaurants and bars around this area. I wasn't sure because the sun was setting, but it looked like in one of the restaurants, a few members of the diving crew from the dive shop were sitting around a table. As I walked closer, it appeared I was right. One of them waved his arm and yelled, "*Hola* Claire, come have a drink with us."

I had to squint a little to see who was talking and realized it was Marcos. He was wearing a white Scuba Mar polo shirt along with the rest of the guys. I smiled and walked toward the group of divers.

"*¡Hola amigos!*" I called out in greeting.

"*¡Hola!* Come have a seat." It was Elena who pulled out a chair next to her.

"*Gracias,*" I said as I sat down next to Elena. My foot brushed against something solid. I thought it was the chair, so I moved my foot back, but the solid object followed my foot.

"What the-" I looked down under the table and saw Luna laying down by my chair.

"Luna! What are you doing here?" I looked at Elena for an explanation.

"I put Luna inside her doghouse because we were closing the shop for the day, but she kept whining. I think she misses Carlos," Elena said as she bent down to pat the little dog.

"I was going to stay back with Luna at the shop, but Marcos told me to bring her. Maybe she will wear herself out being with other people," Elena added.

Marco's logic made sense to me. Besides Luna was behaving well in the outside restaurant, so it was a win-win situation.

"We are just about to have our supper and drinks before we head home. Today we had a large group, and we felt we deserved a drink," said Marcos. In addition to the lead dive master and Elena, there were two other diving guides: Antonio and Felipe.

I already knew Antonio because he was the one who recommended the hostel. But this was the first time I met Felipe. He must have been added to the dive master rotation because there was such a large group of divers today. I remembered the dive shop owner had also told me today's group was a large one, so it made sense they brought in another diving guide.

Typically, each dive master dove with four to six people in their group depending on the experience of the divers. If the group had inexperienced divers, the dive master would take fewer people in the group, so he or she could pay more attention to them. Because Marcos, Carlos, and Antonio were more experienced guides, they would usually take the groups with more people, and leave the junior guides like Felipe to take one or two inexperienced divers. It wasn't like the junior divers weren't as good as the other divers, it was just that it took more experience being responsible for more divers regardless of their diving skill.

I could only imagine the stress of being responsible for another person let alone six other people at a time. Even though I got my rescue diver certification last year, I didn't want to have to use the qualification.

Like most people who got advanced scuba certifications, I enjoyed the academics of scuba diving, and I appreciated learning from more experienced divers.

"So, I heard from another guest at the hostel I am staying at now that you guys dove the Columbia and San Francisco today," I said.

"Yes, that's right! The visibility was amazing and so were the sea creatures," chimed Antonio.

"We saw a large group of eagle rays when we were drifting along the San Francisco reef, and we saw a hammerhead shark in the distance when we were diving along the Columbia," added Felipe.

My jaw dropped open. "Wow! I can't believe that. The last few days I dove, I only saw one hawksbill turtle and a few small sting rays," I cried. "Don't get me wrong, it was still really cool to see the sea life in their element, but I would have loved to see an eagle ray or a hammerhead!"

During the winter months, finding eagle rays is common compared to the summer months. But it was rare to see a hammerhead shark. Normally, these creatures are very shy in the waters off of Cozumel, and they rarely swim close to where the divers are. If a diver spots a hammerhead, it is usually from a distance.

"It was incredible, and it was only the second time I had seen a hammerhead," said Felipe. He had a dreamy look on his face that made me even more envious.

"Would you like something to drink Claire? It's our treat," asked Marcos. "The benefit of having a large group of tourists today was that the tips were greater."

"I would love a drink!" I said at Marco's generosity and added, "I'll take a *limonada.*"

Limonada was essentially the same as a lemonade except it was made with limes. I really wanted another *mojito*, but since I was diving in the morning, I wanted to make sure I was well hydrated. Most people discount how much hydration decreases a diver's chance of being seasick. Early on in my diving journey, an experienced diver told me the trick of not getting seasick was to make sure I was well hydrated and to eat something with carbohydrates that would make my stomach full so the liquid in my stomach would not have room to slosh around. Whether that was actual science or not, I have followed this advice and have never gotten seasick even aboard a small boat. Plus, I already had a *mojito* at the other restaurant.

"I heard people were talking about Drew's death and how they didn't think Carlos killed him," I said trying to steer the conversation to find more information after we ordered drinks.

"Yes, we are in disbelief one of our guests was murdered. Even someone not nice as Drew. We are also completely shocked the police think Carlos did it," answered Marcos. Unlike the dive shop owner, Marcos looked distraught. He kept raking his hand through his hair as he thought about the impossible situation his former coworker was in.

"Yesterday, I saw Carlos being taken away from the police, and I asked *señor Domínguez* if he knew why the police took him. And today, when I went to talk to *señor Dominguez* again, he said someone told the police he saw Carlos grab Drew's arm forcefully, and Drew complained to him. Drew threatened to write a bad review on several tourist websites if the owner did not fire Carlos," I shared the information with the dive crew.

The dive crew didn't seem shocked as I had been when I heard the news. They looked at each other and nodded their heads. It seemed like they already knew this information.

"Do you know why Carlos grabbed Drew's arm?" I probed. Maybe, the guys found out something.

Antonio made a small clearing sound at the back of his throat and said, "well, I didn't hear the conversation between Drew and Carlos, but after Drew walked away, Carlos told me Drew did not leave him a tip."

"What!" I gasped in disbelief and embarrassment. Most

people knew the dive guides earned most of their money from the tips that the guests provided at the end of the trip. Typically, each diver pays about $5-10 dollars per tank to their dive master. So, if the trip was a two-tank dive, then the diver would pay about $10-20 dollars to the crew member. It seemed like a lot of extra money you had to pay on top of the fee for the dive itself, but you were paying for an experienced local diver to guide you to places where it was possible to see interesting sea life. They also made sure you were safe. Although it was extremely rare for divers to die during a scuba diving trip, it sometimes happened.

"I'm stunned Drew didn't leave a tip! Did Carlos say why?" I asked still in amazement over my fellow diver's behavior.

"No, Carlos did not. He was mad, but I don't think he would have actually killed Drew because he didn't leave him a tip," said Antonio. Antonio didn't have to say aloud that even though the dive guides didn't like it when their guests didn't leave a gratuity, it was part of the business. Sometimes, it was because the divers were new to diving with a dive company and didn't know the etiquette, but other times it was because the divers were being rude. As a result, the dive guides had been short-changed before.

A little depressed from not getting more information to help Carlos and feeling a little tired, I decided it was time to go.

"Well, I think I'm turning in for the night. Oh, and Antonio- thank you so much for recommending Maria's place. *La Casa Tranquila* is so neat, and Maria is a wonderful hostess."

"She's really nice, and she was one of the best diving guides on the island before she opened her hostel," Antonio remarked.

"Does she still guide scuba divers?" I asked curiously.

"No, I think she has too much to do at the hostel," Antonio said.

I nodded in understanding. I got up, but before I left the table, I told the crew from Scuba Mar I would be seeing them tomorrow.

"Since I'm here on the island a few more days, I decided to go diving again."

"That's wonderful Claire!" Antonio said. "I'll make sure you are in my group unless Marco claims you for his group." Everyone laughed, and I pretended to be flattered by the attention.

"Aww.. thanks guys. I appreciate you wanting me to be part of your group."

"You're a good diver, and you don't make outrageous demands," Marcos said honestly.

I smiled in embarrassment. My cheeks were red, but in the dim light, it was hard to tell. I didn't know how to respond to the compliment, so I got up. Again, my foot bumped into Luna when I pushed back my chair.

"Hey, Luna, you were so quiet I forgot you were laying down by my feet." Luna stood up and wagged her tail.

"What are you going to do with Luna?"

The crew at Scuba Mar looked at each other but didn't say anything. Finally, Elena spoke up. "I guess I can take Luna back to the dive shop and put her in the doghouse. She would be safe, but I don't think she will like being alone." Elena didn't look happy about leaving the puppy at the shop unattended.

"Do you think Maria would mind if I brought Luna back with me?" I asked Antonio.

"I don't know, but Maria loves animals, and she feeds the stray dogs and cats around the hostel, so I don't think she would mind if you brought Luna with you," Antonio replied.

"That settles it. I'll bring Luna back to my room with me." I bent down to scoop the little chihuahua up. Luna was light as a feather in my arms. As soon as I picked her up, she cuddled against my chest and put her head on my arm.

"Awww..." Elena made a sappy face. "She loves you, Claire."

"I don't know about love, but she certainly does seem comfortable." With Luna in my arms, I couldn't wave goodbye.

"Alright everybody, I guess I'll follow Luna's lead and get ready for bed. I'll see you guys in the morning."

"Adiós, Claire," called out the crew from the shop, but they made no motion to get up from the table. Apparently, they weren't lightweights like me and could stay out later and still get up early the next morning to go diving.

Chapter Twenty-Six

L una's barking interrupted my note taking. She was a good dog and slept most of the morning, but she needed to go out. I looked at my watch.

Hmm... it's only 10:00am. Even though I wasn't scheduled to dive until the afternoon, I decided to head to the dive shop to see what was going on.

I opened the heavy wooden door, and Luna cautiously stepped out. She made her way to the middle of the courtyard and relieved herself next to a tree, which happened to be Fernando's tree.

"*¡Hola!*" He cawed startling both Luna and me. I looked up to see the parrot sitting on his branch. Poor Luna had never come across a parrot before, so she started barking in alarm.

"It's okay, Luna! It's just Fernando." I picked up the little pooch and patted her head to calm her down.

Luna's barking alerted the other guests in their rooms, and they came out to see what was going on.

"Good morning, Claire. Who's this?" Lonnie asked as she walked towards me and the dog.

"Oh, this is Luna."

"What an adorable little dog!" Lonnie put her face close to Luna's and cooed. The puppy could tell the other woman was an admirer because she tilted her little face and wagged her tail.

"Where did you find this cutie?" Lonnie put out her palm for Luna to sniff.

"Luna is a stray, and she has been hanging around Scuba Mar. Carlos, one of the diving guides had been taking care of her, but when the police took him into custody, there was no one to take care of her."

"Oh, is Carlos the one the police think had something to do with that scuba diver's death?" Lonnie asked as she recalled what she had heard on her dive trip.

"Yes, that's correct."

"Poor pup. What are you going to do with Luna? You're not from here, so what will happen when you leave to go back home?"

"I'm not sure Lonnie. I'm going diving this afternoon with Scuba Mar, so I'm going to take Luna with me. Elena, the receptionist, has been watching Luna during the day when everyone is out on the boats, but at night, she has to keep Luna locked up in the doghouse. I took Luna home with me because she doesn't like being alone."

"Do you think the police will release Carlos soon." Lonnie asked thinking about Luna's fate if the guy who had been taking care of her wasn't going to come back.

"Honestly, I don't know." I didn't add I was doing my best to help get Carlos released from jail.

"I hope you find a way to help Carlos or get someone to take care of Luna. I wish I could take her, but I don't want to take her out of the country. Plus, I work crazy hours, so the poor dog would be left alone most of the day." Lonnie patted Luna's head and looked at her wistfully.

"I better get going."

"Of course. I hope you enjoy your dive." Lonnie said and strolled back to her room.

Before I left *La Casa Tranquila*, I went to the guest room to see if there were still some coffee and pastries left over from breakfast.

The door was open, and Maria had laid out more fresh pastries. The smell of the robust Mexican coffee filled the reception room. I put down my mesh bag with my scuba gear next to the same table that Jack and Terry were sitting at the previous day and went to the side bar to help myself with some sweet bread and coffee.

I also grabbed a bowl and poured some water for Luna. The dog lapped the water with her small tongue. I looked to see what I could give her to eat. I didn't see any dog food, but I figured giving her some of the pastries wouldn't hurt.

I broke off a chunk of bread and gave it to Luna before I sat down and bit into the soft and warm dough of the pastry. It was heavenly! I sighed and wondered if Maria made them or bought them every morning. As I chewed my food, I looked out the window to the blue waters of the Caribbean Sea sparkling in the bright sun. Fortunately for me, the wind was calm, so it looked like the ports would not be closed today. With anticipation of the day's dives, I took my empty plate and cup and placed them in a bin underneath the sidebar. Then, I picked up my gear bag and headed out the door.

"Come on Luna!" At the sound of my voice, Luna trailed after me.

The walk to the dive shop didn't take long, and I saw the dive crew loading the boats with the air tanks and the fresh fruit they were going to serve in between the dives. I greeted Elena.

"*¡Hola!*"

"*¡Hola!*" Elena replied. "You're here early."

"Yes, I wanted to walk around the beach and take some

pictures." I gave the receptionist my most innocent look. "Could you watch Luna?"

Luna trotted right up to the receptionist for attention. "Hi, sweetie." Elena reached down to pet the dog. "I'll watch Luna while you are diving."

Whew! Elena didn't suspect anything.

Familiar with the surroundings, Luna wandered off to check out what was going around the shop.

Despite my best intention, I didn't discover anything new about Carlos or Drew's death by arriving early. However, I did get some great photos of the wildlife around the resort and the beach.

I was admiring a picture of an iguana I took on my camera when I spotted Ryan, Aiden, and Peyton standing together with the Tanakas. Because there were only eight guest divers, the owner decided to charter one big boat rather than two smaller boats. This meant that everyone was going to dive together, which was fine because we would be divided into two groups anyway.

"Hey Claire!" Aiden greeted me as he was the first one to spot me.

"Hi everyone!" I gave a small wave.

"I thought you had already left." Aiden had a big grin on his face.

"I was going to leave yesterday, but I decided to stay for a few extra days," I explained.

"That's great!" Aiden seemed genuinely happy to see me, and I could feel a warm rush to my face. I tried to ignore the fact Aiden was still staring at me, so I looked at Peyton.

"How are you doing?" I was facing Peyton, but out of the corner of my eye, I saw Aiden give a small frown. He looked confused when I didn't answer him back.

My stomach dropped. I'm such an idiot. Why didn't I

respond to Aiden before I started a conversation with Peyton. Oh well. Too late.

Not hearing the internal debate that was raging in my head, Peyton replied, "I'm good. Ready to go diving!"

"Me too! How about you guys?" I turned my head back to Aiden and Ryan. I asked them both the question, but I was looking at Aiden trying to make up for the earlier social faux pas.

"It looks like an excellent day for diving," Ryan said looking at the calm water.

"I'm excited to do another day of diving," Aiden said and smiled at me.

Silently telling myself to relax and not to analyze every interaction, I took a deep breath. I found Aiden attractive and fun to be around. I needed to stop being so awkward, so he wouldn't think I was crazy.

"Did you see where we're going today?" I asked them.

"I saw on the whiteboard the boat is taking us to the Palancar Horseshoe and Delilah reefs," Ryan volunteered this information.

"That's awesome. I love the Palancars!" Peyton said excited by the prospect of diving the big reef formations. Before I could agree with Peyton, Marcos came out of the dive shop with a clipboard in his hand.

"Okay, everyone, we are ready for you to get on the boat," Marcos called out to the guests waiting on the pier.

"Hello Claire," Tom and Margaret said as they got in line.

"Hello, how are you?" I replied

"We're happy to go diving, but we're sad this is our last day," Margaret answered for herself and her husband.

"Was Cozumel everything you thought it was going to be?"

"Yes, and more! The only bad part was when that diver died." Margaret shook her head. She looked upset, but her husband had a dark look on his face.

"What do you think Tom?"

"I agree with Margaret," he said and stepped in the boat.

Tom's behavior was odd, but I didn't have time to ask him more questions. People were waiting to get in the boat.

I picked up my mesh bag and climbed in after Margaret.

I was excited like my diving buddies to go back to the Palancar reef, but I was anxious because I hadn't found a way to bring up the situation regarding Carlos. I only had a few days to solve Drew's death and get Carlos out of jail because I couldn't afford to change my flight again.

Chapter Twenty-Seven

Giving an okay signal to Antonio I was ready to go, I took a giant stride into the clear, blue water with one hand covering my mask and the regulator in my mouth. As soon as I hit the water, I bounced back to the surface. I waited until everyone was in the water and then looked to Antonio for his signal to descend. One by one, each diver disappeared under water as we released the air in our BCD with the inflator hose.

As I slowly sank, I made sure I swallowed to equalize my ears. Scuba diving was very safe, but one of the ways that someone could get injured was if they didn't clear the pressure from their ears as they increased in depth. It was something divers needed to do frequently until they reached the depth that they were going to be diving at.

In Cozumel, the dive masters usually start at the deepest depth and let the divers explore the area before slowly gaining elevation during the dive. This way the divers could enjoy the marine life and structure without ascending and descending to different depths and wasting precious air. The dive masters were so experienced in this that the divers didn't realize a path was choreographed through the reefs for their maximum enjoyment.

On this dive to the Palancar horseshoe, Antonio drifted along the wall of the reef and pointed out sea creatures that were hiding in the ledges with his high-powered flashlight. As we were about to go through the first swim through, Antonio tapped against his air tank to get all the divers' attention. With his hand, he gestured towards the bottom where there was a sandy patch in between the reef formation.

At first, I couldn't tell what Antonio was pointing at, but then Aiden started to flail his arms excitedly. Since he was right behind Antonio, he was the first diver to see the nurse shark that was resting underneath the ledge. He put one hand straight up on top of his head which was the hand signal for sighting a shark. That got everyone else excited.

Even though I had seen a nurse shark before, the sight of any sea creature in real life never got old. When it was my turn to swim by the shark's resting place, I swam a little closer, so I could take a few pictures and video with my underwater camera.

My camera wasn't the most expensive one on the market, but with an adequate flash, I was able to get some memorable souvenirs of the diving trips I went on. One thing I learned over the years was that it wasn't necessarily the quality of the equipment but the skill of the operator that made the difference in how a picture or video turned out.

I flipped the setting from picture to video and trained my camera on the nurse shark and held the button for ten seconds before releasing it. I was amazed to see the shark resting in our vicinity for such a long time, and I was able to film the encounter before the shark swam away. I prayed when I got to the boat and re-examined my video, I had taken a good quality video to share with my friends.

In addition to the shark, we spotted a hawksbill turtle during our dive through the Palancar horseshoe reef. And as a final treat, during our three-minute safety stop, we saw a large group of spotted eagle rays swimming past us about ten meters away. Peyton was the first to spot the graceful creatures as she was swimming closest to them.

She rapped her knuckles on the aluminum tank to get our attention. When we looked at her, she pointed down at the graceful rays swimming underneath us. I quickly turned on my camera and tried to get video of the gentle creatures before they completely left my field of view. Then, the three minutes were up, and we continued our ascent.

To our great luck, Juan and Rafa were circling the waters near us when we surfaced, so we didn't have to wait long to be pulled out of the water. I could see the other group diving with Marcos was already on the boat. I looked at my dive computer and noted my bottom time was 58 minutes, which was a decent amount of time under water. I would have loved to stay a little longer as most divers would as well, but I was happy our group saw the shark along with the turtle and the spotted eagle rays.

After Rafa pulled us into boat, Ryan told Marcos and the other divers about the sea life we encountered.

"It was amazing! The nurse shark was only a few feet away, and it stayed under the ledge for a long time. I thought it would swim away when we passed by it."

The Tanakas and another couple that were in Marcos's group groaned in disappointment when they heard about the shark. One man who brought with him an expensive camera sighed dramatically and rolled his eyes because even though he was lugging around a costly piece of equipment; it didn't guarantee him an interesting sea life encounter.

"I have a $3000 camera, and the most exciting thing I saw was an angelfish." I understood the man's disappointment because there were many times I went diving and didn't see anything of interest.

Before I returned to my seat on the side bench, I stopped at the freshwater bucket and gently placed my camera and flash into the pail to rinse off the salt water. Then I sat on the plastic bench waiting for Rafa to come my way with some snacks.

While we were underwater, Rafa and Juan had cut up some fresh pineapple and cantaloupe to serve to the guests when we came up.

"Would you like some fruit?" Rafa asked when he finally got to where I was sitting.

"I would love some." I reached and grabbed a few pineapple spears and cantaloupe slices. *"Gracias."*

Rafa smiled, and he moved to serve the others.

We munched on the refreshing snacks as Juan motored to the second destination. The sun was out in full strength, so I was able to warm up in no time, and the ride to the next reef gave me time to think more about who the possible suspects could be.

"Hi Claire, did you enjoy the dive?" I looked up to see Aiden standing in front of me. I scooted over on the bench to make room for him.

"It was awesome! I'm so glad we saw the shark, turtle, and the rays today because the last two times I dove, I didn't see anything but a small sea turtle."

Aiden sat down and nodded in agreement. "I'm glad you stayed a few more days. I really wanted to talk to you more, and the last time we spoke was the day Elena found Drew's body."

I shuddered as I recalled the events of that day. "It was surreal, and I can't believe Drew is dead. How do you think he died? Do you think that someone killed him?" I held my breath waiting for his answer and hoped he didn't think Carlos was connected any way with Drew's death.

"I don't know," Aiden replied as he shook his head in puzzlement. "I mean-there were plenty of people that didn't like him, but I don't think that anyone would go out of their way to kill him."

"Did you know that he stiffed the crew a tip on his last day?" I asked.

"No, but that doesn't surprise me because he was an—"

"Jerk," I said finishing his sentence. Aiden was going to use another word, but I was trying to be respectful of the dead man.

"Exactly!" Aiden agreed.

"Do you think one of the dive crew could have killed Drew?" I asked hesitantly trying to see if Aiden suspected anything.

"Do I think one of the crew would kill someone over a stiffed tip? I doubt it, but I don't know for sure. I know the crew depends on the gratuity to supplement their income, but I don't think it makes or breaks them in terms of their overall day's wages unless Drew didn't tip them at all for any of the days that he dove with the company." We both frowned when we realized it was possible that Drew may not have left the crew anything after his multiple days of diving.

"Hey- what are you guys talking about?" Peyton asked as she and Ryan walked to where Aiden and I were sitting.

"We were talking about Drew, and how he didn't tip the crew after his dives and whether that might have been a motive for someone to kill him," I explained.

"I think it's terrible Drew died, but I can honestly say he wasn't a great guy to be around. Did you know he tried to hit on me when he first met me?" Peyton asked.

Aiden and I shared a look. Although we didn't hear the conversation, we saw Peyton walking away.

"I didn't know he was flirting with you, but I can believe it because he tried to make a pass at me as well," I said.

"He did?" Aiden asked. He narrowed his eyes in disapproval. For some reason, Aiden's reaction made me happy because I knew it bothered Aiden that another guy tried to hit on me.

"Yes, that's before he told me I needed to lose some weight."

Peyton and the guys looked at me in disbelief.

"Did you know Drew had the audacity to tell me his dive computer was better than mine?" Tom and his wife joined our conversation.

"No, but that sounds like something he would say." I slumped my shoulders. Drew didn't endear himself with others while he was alive.

We didn't have more time to talk about the dead man because the ride to the Delilah reef was short. However, we didn't immediately get ready to dive because we still had residual nitrogen in our bloodstream and needed to wait a little longer before we went underwater.

According to my dive computer we still had about fifteen minutes left on the surface interval before we could dive. The surface interval was the time spent above water in between dives that allowed the nitrogen to dissolve from the body. The time was calculated by the amount of time a diver spent in the water at the deepest depth before ascending.

The other divers in my group probably had the same amount of surface time left, but since each person absorbs and releases nitrogen at a different rate, the surface time would vary among the divers by a minute or two.

Soon the symbol that looked like a battery on my dive watch turned green from yellow indicating the nitrogen level in my body was safe for me to do my second dive. I already had my wetsuit on, but I needed to put on my BCD. During the ride to the second reef, Rafa switched the used-up air tank with a full one, so all I had to do was turn on the air valve to make sure the air flowed into my BCD without any leaks. To my satisfaction, I saw I had 3300 pounds of air in my gauge.

I walked over to Antonio and let him know I was ready. "Antonio, I'm good to go for my second dive."

"Great! How about everyone else." The diver master looked at the others.

"We're good too," said Aiden and Ryan.

Peyton gave Antonio a thumbs up signaling she was ready to dive.

With our group huddled around him, Antonio gave the instructions for the dive. "Okay, we'll head down to forty feet and drift on top of the reef. There are a lot of beautiful things to see, and we should be able to dive for over an hour this time, but if you run low on air, signal to me that you and your buddy are going to ascend. Again, don't go below me or ahead of me. *¿Sí?*"

"*¡Sí!*" We replied as we formed a line at the back of the boat to jump into the water with Juan's help.

Similar to the Palancar horseshoe reef, the visibility of the Delilah reef was incredible. I thought I was able to see at least 90 feet away. However, the current was stronger on top of the reef, and I was not protected by the swim throughs and the reef wall. As a result, the other divers and myself zoomed through the water, and I barely had time to look around me before I flew to the next part of the reef.

Although there were no interesting structures to swim through, the variety of fish were astounding along with the different types of sponges and coral. I kept my camera on the video setting as I drifted along trying to relax as much as possible to control my breathing. Even though it wasn't a competition, I did not want to be the first person to signal that I was low on air.

Up ahead, Antonio tried to slow down by moving his arms against the current as he swam towards a rock formation and pointed his flashlight at the creature trying its best not to be noticed. When I drifted closer, I saw the black and white striped face and a glimpse of yellow which I thought might be the elusive splendid toad fish that could only be found in the waters off of Cozumel and *Isla Mujer*, which was another island located off the coast of Cancun.

I trained my camera on the fish with one hand and pumped my other hand above me in excitement. I had to check my video when I downloaded the images from the camera, but I was positive it was the splendid toad fish.

We drifted along some more, and this time, I took video of Aiden, Ryan, Peyton, and Antonio. I only met these folks on this trip, but I rapidly connected with them as I got to know them on the boat ride to and from the dive sites. I hoped I would stay in touch with them through social media. And since it appeared Aiden might be interested in me, I hoped I got a chance to see him again after this trip.

As I filmed them, they made funny faces and poised in the water. Soon, Aiden signaled to the group he reached the designated low air limit first. All the goofing around in the water made him go through the air fast.

I had another 500 pounds of air before I reached the low air limit, but I decided to ascend with Aiden and Ryan. I signaled to Peyton that I wanted to go up. She nodded and gave me an okay sign. Antonio saw his group was ready to go up, so he gave the hand signal to ascend. When we reached fifteen feet, we stopped for our three-minute safety stop. After my watch beeped to let me know that the safety stop was complete, I kicked my fins slowly to propel myself to the surface. This time, we were not so lucky, and Juan's boat was not within sight, so we had to flag down another boat to request on the radio for Juan to come find us.

With my BCD fully inflated, I leaned back and floated in the water. The water was fairly calm, so there were no large waves that would make me seasick. I looked at the blue sky above me, and the thoughts surrounding Drew's death came back. I started to feel a little anxious again because I still hadn't found anything useful to help free Carlos. I kept getting these nagging feelings something was not quite right. I was supposed to leave the day after tomorrow, but I was nowhere close to finding out who really killed Drew.

Chapter Twenty-Eight

Back on the boat, I tugged my wetsuit completely off and put on my fleece robe. The sun was still bright, so it was still very warm on the surface, but after spending almost an hour underneath the water, I was chilled to the bone. The fluffy robe soon warmed me up, and I leaned against the plastic bench and looked out towards the sea as I drank from my bottled water. Breathing the gas mixture from the dive tank always made my throat extremely dry. I was also getting hungry, but there was no fresh fruit on the way back. However, I told myself when we got back to the pier, I would return to the small restaurant I ate at yesterday. It was also near the same place that I ran into Marcos and Antonio, so I asked my dive group if they wanted to join me.

"Do you guys want to go out to dinner? I went to an excellent little restaurant where they served the best lionfish tacos."

"I heard of them, but I have never eaten one," Peyton said, and she definitely seemed game to try.

"Neither have I," Aiden and Ryan echoed.

"Bueno," Antonio said coming beside us. "That means that you have to try one before you leave the island."

"Antonio, would you like to join us?" I asked.

"I would love to," he replied.

"Anyone else who wants to join us is welcome too," I said. The other people in Marco's group declined saying they already had plans for dinner.

"What about you Marcos?" Peyton asked the lead dive guide.

"Thanks, but I have to get home to my wife. It's her birthday, and I'm taking her to some place special." Marcos explained while he started to put away the gear on the boat.

"That's nice." Peyton said. "I hope you and your wife have a wonderful time."

"I hope so too because I'm taking her someplace very expensive," Marcos said and winked to let us know he was joking.

We laughed and agreed that after we got back to the dock, we would quickly clean our gear and freshen up before we met at the restaurant. I also mentioned whoever got to the restaurant first should reserve a table for all of us.

With a plan set for dinner, we enjoyed the remainder of the boat ride back to the resort dock. A few minutes later, when Juan pulled his boat next to the dock, there was a mad scramble to get off the boat and clean up. Unlike Aiden, Ryan, and Peyton who only had to walk back to their rooms at the resort, I had to walk with my gear back to *La Casa Tranquila*.

I was about to go to the dive shop office to get Luna, but the dog was already at the pier waiting for me.

"What a good dog!" I said and picked her up for a hug.

Luna gave a short bark and wagged her tail.

"Claire, can you take Luna with you again?" It was Elena. She came out of the office when she heard Luna bark.

"I think so. I haven't asked Maria if I could keep her with me, but if Antonio is right, I don't think she will mind."

"Great! I'm about to close the shop, and I wasn't sure what to do with Luna," Elena said looking at the little dog that was curled up in my arms.

"No problem," I said to Elena as I set down Luna and picked up my gear bag.

"By the way, a few of us are going out to dinner, do you want to join us?"

Elena looked surprised but happy at the invitation. "That's so nice of you to ask Claire, and I would love to, but I have to go help my mother move some furniture around. She just moved in with me after my father died."

"I'm so sorry about your dad. When did he pass away?"

"He died from cancer a few months ago in Guadalajara, but my mother didn't want to leave right after his death."

"I understand, and again, I'm so sorry!" I said to Elena and gave her a hug. She nodded in thanks and hugged me back.

"I wish I could go with you guys, but I hope you enjoy your meal," Elena said and I picked up my gear again.

"Okay, let's go!" I said and patted my hand on my leg for Luna to follow me. "*Ciao*, Elena!"

"Thanks Claire!" Elena waved at me and walked back to the resort.

"You're welcome! Have a fun time with your mom," I said over my shoulder as I speed-walked to the hostel with Luna trailing after me.

In a world record pace, I rushed to clean my gear in the shower and laid it out on the tile floor next to the window to let it dry. Then I strode back to the bathroom to rinse the salt water with my scented shampoo and soap. I dressed in some cutoff jean shorts and a tank top and wondered if I should bother fixing my hair. But I figured since Aiden had seen me when I came out of the water with my hair splayed all over my face, how I fixed my hair wouldn't matter. I brushed my shoulder length hair and put it into a low ponytail. "Good enough!" I said as I examined myself in the bathroom mirror.

Fifteen minutes later, I locked the door to my room and walked with Luna towards the back fence that led to the beach path to the restaurant. Along the way, I spotted the bright red and green parrot in one of the trees in the courtyard. In greeting, the parrot squawked "*¡Hola!*"

"*¡Hola!*" I sang back. Luna gave a short bark for her greeting to Fernando.

By the time Luna and I got to the restaurant, we were the last to arrive, but the group didn't mind waiting as they were sitting around two tables that were pushed together and drinking *mojitos* and eating chips.

"*Hola* Claire!" Antonio stood up from his chair and waved at me to get my attention.

Aiden quickly stood up and pulled out the empty chair between him and Antonio. "*Gracias*!" I smiled in thanks. As I sat down, I could smell the soap he used.

"*De nada*!" Aiden replied and smiled back.

"Hey, who is this?" Peyton noticed Luna who was standing next to me.

"This is Luna. She's a stray that has been hanging around the dive shop. Between Elena and I, we have been taking care of her until Carlos gets out of police custody."

"Did Carlos adopt her?" Ryan asked as he petted Luna on her head.

"I don't know. Elena never said." I shrugged.

"Have you ordered food already?" I asked as I looked around the table.

"No. We wanted to wait for you, but we ordered drinks," Peyton said.

I flagged down the waitress and ordered water and a *mojito*. In my humble opinion, not only did this restaurant have the best tacos, but it also made the most delicious *mojitos*. The refreshing drink was heavenly- it had just the right amount of rum, mint, and lime to balance the sugar.

When the waitress came back with my drinks, we all ordered the lionfish tacos, but I worried what I could give Luna.

"*Perdón*, am I allowed to order something for my dog?" I gestured to Luna who was peacefully laying down by my feet.

The waitress looked at Luna, noticing her for the first time. She broke out into a wide smile and said, *"¡Por supuesto!* You can order just the grilled fish meat."

"Wonderful- I'll do that." Luna was such a good dog, and I had really taken to her, but I knew I couldn't bring her back with me. I hoped I could find a way to get Carlos out of jail.

Before I finished my *mojito*, the waitress came back with our food. As we sat around the table eating and drinking, we reminisced over our afternoon dives which let us to talking about the other places we had dove.

"What's your favorite place that you have ever dove?" Peyton asked.

"Cozumel!" Aiden and I said at the same time.

"I have never dove there, but I really want to dive in the Red Sea," answered Ryan.

"The Mexican *cenotes,*" Antonio said deftly.

"*Cenotes*?" Peyton asked. "What are *cenotes*?"

"*Cenotes* are big sinkholes that are filled with water," Antonio explained. "Mexico is part of the Yucatan peninsula which is made from soft limestone. Over time, the parts of the limestone crumbled away leaving large sinkholes around the country. These sinkholes are filled with fresh water that many Mexicans use every day."

"Where are the *cenotes* located?" Aiden asked intrigued by what he heard. He was interested in the history and geology, but he was also excited to know more about diving in a sinkhole.

"There are actually quite a few in Mexico, and many of them are located right across the sea from us in Tulum. Many divers will book a trip to Tulum to visit the Mayan ruins and also arrange for a *cenote* dive," Antonio replied.

"What level of certification do you need to dive in a *cenote*? Do you need to be cave diving certified?" I asked. I had heard about *cenotes* on my previous diving trips to Cozumel, but I didn't think about diving them because I didn't like dark spaces. I was terrified at the thought of losing my way and running out of air. It wasn't common, but there were a few people that died while cave diving because they ran out of air and couldn't find their way out of the caves. Those people ended up being the cautionary tale that scuba diving instructors would tell their students when they wanted to remind the students to not dive past their limits.

"For most of the *cenotes*, you don't have to be cave dive certified," Antonio replied, "but there are a few that require advanced diving skills and experience."

He looked at the dejected faces around the table and said, "but you don't have to have cave dive training. You can always dive the cavern part which is the opening of the cave." Antonio's explanation made the guys feel better as he continued, "in fact, I used to work for a dive shop in Tulum that took divers on guided *cenote* tours before I moved to Cozumel."

"Why did you move to Cozumel?" Peyton asked as I wondered the same thing.

"Well, you can make more money working for dive shops that go to the reefs than to the *cenotes* because more people can dive in the sea than in the small sinkholes. Plus, a lot of divers are not interested in diving in the dark," Antonio replied.

"That would be me," I piped up and shuddered at the thought of being trapped in an enclosed space with no air.

"*Cenotes* are smaller and darker than the Caribbean Sea, but they have a unique beauty to themselves," said Antonio with a smile. "Even though, I don't work for the dive company in Tulum anymore, I still arrange tours for guests that are in Cozumel and want to try *cenote* diving."

"Really?" Aiden asked. "That would be awesome if you could set something up for Ryan and me. We have a few more days here in Cozumel, and we were going to keep diving in the sea, but this would be a great opportunity to try something new. Are you interested, Ryan?" He looked at his friend.

"Count me in!" Ryan said speaking in between bites of chips.

"Speaking of which, how much is it?" Aiden asked.

Before Antonio could answer, Peyton chimed in, "I would love to go to if it's the same price as the boat dives."

"It's a little more expensive than the resort's two tank dives, but the fee covers the ferry trip from Cozumel to La Playa Del Carmen and the jeep ride to the *cenote*," Antonio said. "It also includes the weights, tanks, snacks, and water. If you want, I can make reservations for tomorrow or the day after."

"Let's make it the day after," Aiden said as he looked to Ryan and Peyton to see if they agreed with the plan. Both nodded back in affirmation. "Claire, we would ask if you would be interested but since you leave the day after tomorrow and don't like dark and small spaces, I'm assuming you don't want to go."

I laughed and said, "at some point, I'm going to find the courage to dive the *cenotes*, but since I'm scheduled to fly out on the same day that you all want to go, I'll have to wait for another time."

Maybe it was the *mojitos* or just being out in the fresh air, but I felt really outgoing and said uncharacteristically, "you know, I really enjoyed diving with you guys even though we just met on this trip. We should keep in touch and maybe in the future, we can meet up somewhere to dive together." I cringed a little after I expressed the sentiments. I hoped I didn't sound like I was desperate to have friends, but I saw everyone was nodding.

"That's a great idea!" Peyton said. "I usually come to Mexico with my parents because they love the food and the warm weather, but my parents don't dive, and I'm the only child, so it's nice to be able to have someone I know to dive with."

I nodded in understanding. "I'm an only child too, and I

don't know anyone in my immediate group of friends that know or like to scuba dive. It's too bad because they don't know what they are missing." I sighed as I thought about Julia declaring she didn't want to dive again after she got certified.

"Let's exchange social media account names, and we can follow each other," Ryan suggested.

"I'll post the pictures and videos I took and tag you guys," I said.

"Thank you- that would be terrific. I don't have a camera yet, but it's on my list of gear I want to buy. Scuba diving equipment is sooo expensive, and it's taking me forever to buy my own stuff," Peyton bemoaned.

"I'm finding that out as well. I thought the most expensive part was to get certified. I figured I could rent the gear when I dove. However, I noticed the rental gear doesn't always fit right, and I would like to have my own dive computer to keep track of my dives," Ryan said.

I nodded in agreement with Ryan and Peyton that the scuba diving equipment was expensive, and it took time to acquire the necessary items. But in my mind, it was worth every penny to have your own gear, so you could be familiar with the set up. When your life depended on the equipment, you wanted to be sure it was properly maintained and fit correctly.

We sat around enjoying the approaching sunset. It was times like this I was grateful to be able to have the opportunity to travel and experience new sights. Even though I would have made more money as an engineer like my mother wanted me to be, I wouldn't have had the time to travel when I wanted. As a teacher, I had lengthy breaks in between teaching positions and during school holidays that allowed me to travel and stay longer if I wanted to.

For the bachelorette weekend, Julia took a few days off, but that was all she could manage because she needed to save the rest of her vacation days for her wedding and the honeymoon. I couldn't imagine only having two weeks off like Julia during the year to travel.

When the last lionfish taco was eaten, I yawned without thinking. "Excuse me! I didn't realize how tired I was."

"Don't worry about it. I feel the same way. I think it's being out in the sun all day and then having these drinks," Peyton replied as she yawned herself.

"After hearing you guys plan your trip to the *cenote*, I am a little envious and wish I was going with you," I sighed wistfully.

"Don't worry Claire, you will have to come back to Cozumel and try it," Antonio said.

"So, how do you want us to pay for the trip?" Ryan asked practically. "Do we pay you or the tour group in Tulum?"

"You can pay me, and I have to ask that you pay in advance because I had an incident where someone said he was going to pay me back, and he never did. I ended up losing 5,000 pesos due to this person's dishonesty."

"I can't believe someone would do that. What a jerk." I blanched at the thought of not paying.

"Yes, you can say *señor* Drew was that," Antonio said ruefully.

"Drew!" We said in unison.

"*¡Sí!* Drew was the guy who asked me to set up a tour for him and one other person to the *cenote*. After I reserved the tour and paid for it up front because the tour company in Tulum needed the money to arrange for a jeep to pick them up at the ferry terminal at La Playa Del Carmen, he and his friend never showed up.

The next day, when I saw *señor* Drew on the Scuba Mar charter, I asked him why he never showed up. My friend at the *cenote* company called and chewed me out for reserving a tour for guests that didn't show up. *Señor* Drew shrugged and said his friend couldn't make it, so he didn't want to go alone. I said that was fine, but why didn't he call and let me know that I should cancel the trip. I also told him he still owed me money for the trip which he replied that he wasn't going to pay because he didn't go on the trip." Antonio told the astonishing story to us.

"I can't believe what I am hearing!" I cried out in dismay.

"So that's what Drew was asking me to go on," Peyton said as it dawned on her the conversation she had with the dead diver as the others looked at her questioningly. "A couple of days ago, Drew asked me if I was interested in diving a *cenote* with him. At the time, I didn't know what a *cenote* was, and I wasn't interested in diving whatever it was with him anyway, so I said no." She explained more in detail what happened.

"He must have assumed you would say yes, and that was why he went ahead and asked Antonio to reserve the tour," Ryan mused.

"It was probably unfathomable to someone like Drew anyone could resist his charms." Peyton grimaced at the thought of going on a date with a guy who was as narcissistic as Drew.

The guys and Peyton were too busy making comments about Drew's prowess that they didn't observe Antonio's face. The anger he held in restraint became more apparent as the guys piled more criticism against the dead American.

Without any warning, Antonio stood up from the table. "Sorry guys, but I have to go and check out some stuff for tomorrow's dive." Without waiting for us to reply, he hastily took out some bills from his pocket of his shorts and threw them down on the table leaving us with our mouths open in surprise.

Chapter Twenty-Nine

I was stumped by the way Antonio reacted when he told us Drew canceled the *cenote* trip that he had reserved for him. On the other hand, it made sense because losing several hundred dollars of his own wasn't a great feeling.

I waited until Antonio was out of earshot, and then asked, "did you guys notice Antonio's expression when he mentioned Drew didn't pay him for arranging the *cenote* dive tour?"

"Not really," Peyton said as she tried to recall how Antonio looked over dinner.

"He was really agitated telling us the story about Drew."

"Now that you mentioned it, I wonder if Antonio also spoke to Drew right before he died." Aiden's comment made all four of us look at each other with the realization that maybe Antonio had something to do with Drew's death.

"Do you guys think Antonio killed Drew?" Peyton asked voicing what we had been thinking.

"It's hard to believe someone would kill another person over a canceled reservation," Ryan said in disbelief.

"But it wasn't a canceled reservation," I clarified. "If Drew had canceled, Antonio could have called the tour company and canceled the tour so he could get some of his money back. Instead, Drew just ghosted him."

"Still, it's hard to believe someone would go to that extreme," Aiden said unconvinced Antonio would do something so drastic.

"I would normally agree with you, but 5,000 Mexican Pesos is a lot of money for the dive guides. You know they only make about $20 US a day from the dive shop, and they have to make the rest off of tips. If Antonio lost over $250 dollars due to Drew's inconsideration, it would have taken awhile for Antonio to earn that kind of money back. Plus, we don't know what kind of financial situation Antonio was in the first place." I didn't want to sound pushy, but I wanted to make sure my friends who were fairly new to the diving community understood how the divers in Mexico got paid.

There was silence at the table after I finished telling them about the diving industry, so I decided it was a good time to end things for the day.

"I better head back to the hostel and get some rest."

"Yeah, I better go check in with my parents and let them know I signed up for a *cenote* tour." Peyton said. "They are going to hyperventilate when I tell them about diving in a sinkhole. They already think diving in the open water is dangerous enough."

After we paid for the food, we walked together on the beach path with Luna strolling smartly next to me.

"I can't believe how well-behaved Luna is," remarked Peyton.

"Isn't she great? I wish I could keep her, but as an international English teacher, I have to move a lot, so having a dog even as small as Luna isn't a good idea." I frowned at the thought of leaving Luna behind.

Before we knew it, we were by the beach entrance of the resort. Thinking everyone was going to go their separate ways, I waved goodbye to my friends and continued to walk along the beach path to *La Casa Tranquila*.

I didn't get very far when Aiden stopped me in my tracks and said, "what are you doing tomorrow?" I know you have another day on the island before heading back to the States."

"Uh..." I was unsure whether I should tell Aiden about the real reason I was staying a few extra days on Cozumel. He heard the hesitation in my voice and thought I wasn't interested in spending more time with him, so he said quickly, "you probably already have plans."

Aiden looked embarrassed, so I decided to tell him the truth because I didn't want him to think I was rejecting him. "No, no-that's not it." I took a deep breath. "This is probably going to sound unbelievable, but I'm trying to find out who really killed Drew, so I can help Carlos get out of jail."

Aiden was astonished by my revelation. "You are trying to solve a crime? I thought you were an English teacher?"

"I am an English teacher, but I don't like when I come across something that I think is wrong. In this case, I don't think Carlos had anything to do with Drew's death, but he was taken to jail anyways. And no one can tell me why he is a suspect," I added in frustration.

I thought Aiden was going to tell me I was crazy for extending my stay to help someone I barely knew, but he surprised me. "You know what? I'm going to help you figure out what happened to Drew. I'm mean if that's okay with you." Aiden stared at me waiting for my response.

"Really?" I asked. I put my hand on my chest in surprise "You don't think I'm nuts trying to help Carlos by finding out who killed Drew."

"No, I don't think you're nuts. I don't know Carlos well, but I thought he was a decent guy, and I think it's really nice you want to help him. Plus, I'm an attorney, and I can help him if he needs representation if he's being held illegally. And this way, I can spend more time with you." Aiden added the last part in a rush.

I smiled at his sweet comment, but I was too self-conscious to directly address it. Instead, I said, "that would be great if you could help me." I hoped Aiden would take my affirmation as a sign I wanted to spend more time with him too.

"Okay then. What do you want to do first?" Aiden asked.

"Why don't we meet back here tomorrow morning to talk to Antonio again. There was something strange about the way he acted over dinner when he told us about Drew and the *cenote* dive," I said as I thought about Antonio's explanation.

"Sounds good. Why don't we meet at the pier at 7:30 before the dive boat leaves for its first trip of the day," Aiden agreed.

"Good idea." Since we just made plans for the next morning, there was nothing else we needed to do. I started to feel a little awkward standing there, so I reached out to give Aiden a hug and tell him goodbye. But as I moved to raise my arms towards him, Aiden leaned down to hug me at the same time, so I ended up slapping him in the face with my right palm.

"Oh my gosh- I'm so sorry!" I was mortified, but Aiden laughed and said, "that will teach me for trying to give you a hug goodbye."

I wanted to melt into the path, but I told myself not to act like I was thirteen.

"Ha- you better watch out! I took two years of judo in college, so I can defend myself from unwanted advances." I joked and added "Okay, I'm going to give you a hug now, so don't make any sudden movements."

This time, I managed to bring both arms up without hitting Aiden in the face to give him a hug. In return, he brought my body closer than most friends would have done, so it confirmed my suspicion that Aiden was indeed interested in me more than just a friend. After the hug, which lasted a few seconds longer than necessary, Aiden let me go. My face started to flush, so I

DEATH ON COZUMEL ISLAND

took a few paces back hoping he wouldn't notice my uncomfortableness.

Luckily, he didn't, and said "I guess I will see you tomorrow." Then, he bent down to pet Luna. "Bye, Luna!"

I waited until Aiden stopped petting the dog and then said, "sounds like a plan. I hope you have a good night." I gave him one last wave as I continued my way to *La Casa Tranquila*.

Walking on the beach with Luna, I noticed it was a beautiful evening. The smooth water reflected the stars in the sky. But I was too distracted by the earlier conversation to really appreciate the scenery. Things with Aiden were going in an interesting direction. My stomach fluttered as I recalled our hug.

However, my giddiness faded as my thoughts turned to Antonio. *There has got to be more to the story*, I thought in frustration. I was glad Aiden was going with me to the dive shop to talk to Antonio just in case he was involved with Drew's death.

As I thought about the situation more, I recalled there were people that witnessed Drew and Carlos having an argument, but no one saw if Drew also had an angry confrontation with Antonio. So many questions were left unanswered that I started to get a headache.

I looked down at the little dog keeping pace with me.

"Luna, we have got to get to the bottom of this and help free Carlos. Otherwise, I don't know what is going to happen to you." When I first decided to help Carlos, it was because I thought Carlos was unjustly taken into custody, but now, I really wanted to help him, so Luna would not be left stranded.

Chapter Thirty

The cellphone alarm beeped alerting me it was time to get up. It was only 6:30 in the morning, but the sun was already shining brightly into my room. I almost pulled the covers over my head and went back to sleep after I turned off the alarm when I realized I had to get to the dive shop early before the other guests arrived. I wanted to make sure I could talk to Antonio without anyone listening to my questions. I had taken a quick shower yesterday after I returned from dinner to get rid of the sweat from the ever-present humidity, so I didn't have to do much this morning to get ready.

After I locked the door with the heavy iron key, I headed to the reception room where I hoped Maria had at least a pot of coffee available. I discovered during my college years if I wanted to function, I had to have coffee first thing in the morning. I saw that the door to the reception room was wide open, and there was a fragrant smell of rich coffee coming from inside.

"Thank you, Maria!" I muttered as I grabbed a colorful ceramic mug and poured some hot coffee into it. The coffee had a spicy smell, and to my delight, when I took a sip of the drink, I could taste the sweet cinnamon that cut the bitterness of the dark roast. "Wow! This is delicious."

I had to ask Maria where she got this coffee so I could bring some home with me. In fact, I thought I might buy a bag of coffee beans for Julia as a souvenir from the bachelorette weekend.

Even though I wanted to sit by the window and enjoy my coffee, I forced myself to gulp the hot liquid as fast as I could. It might have been the caffeine, but my heart was racing at the thought of finding out if Antonio had anything to do with Drew's death. I hoped he didn't because he was a thoughtful and considerate person, but it was important I find information that could set Carlos free. With that thought, I took one final swig of coffee. I regretted I couldn't have a second cup, but time was running out. I put the mug underneath the sideboard in a rubber tub that Maria used to collect the used dishes.

"Sorry Luna, but I don't have any breakfast for you. Here's some water, and maybe later after we talk to Antonio, Aiden and I can find something for you to eat." I said this to Luna as she was a human that could respond. The dog cocked her head to one side and looked at me as if to say, "that sounds like a good plan."

I put the bowl Luna used to drink water under the sideboard after she was done, and then we headed to the back of the hostel as I decided the beach path was the quickest route to the dive shop. The sunlight was so brilliant I had to dig in my purse to find my sunglasses. As I walked towards the dive shop, I saw there weren't a lot of people on the path. With the end of the winter break for most Americans, there were considerably less people today than there were just yesterday on the island.

In no time at all, I could see the dock the dive shop used to load its guests. There was only one boat waiting to be loaded with passengers and their gear. I picked up the pace of my stride when I saw Marcos and the owner talking. I wondered what they were talking about.

"*Buenos dias, señores!*" I chirped. I grimaced slightly thinking my greeting sounded a little fake.

The two men stopped talking and looked to see who was walking towards them. "Is everything okay?" I asked when I stopped in front of them and saw their troubled expressions.

"Antonio has not shown up to work this morning, and he isn't answering his cellphone." Marcos said.

"We have a small group today, but we need another guide because one of the guests has paid for a private guide. If Antonio doesn't show up in a few minutes, I'm going to have to call another dive guide to come instead," *Señor Domínguez* added.

"Maybe he just has his cellphone turned off, and he is running late," I offered. I really hoped Antonio would show up soon because I wanted to talk to him as well. At that moment, I saw Aiden heading toward us from the resort. He was smiling until he saw my anxious look.

"What's wrong?" Aiden asked me, gently putting a hand on my shoulder.

"Antonio hasn't come into work yet," I replied. We looked at each other, and in our minds, Antonio's absence made him seem more likely he could be involved in Drew's death. I hoped and prayed Antonio didn't have anything to do with Drew, but his disappearance was suspicious.

"Has Antonio ever shown up late or missed work?" I asked to fill the void as we stood around waiting to see if the dive guide would make his appearance.

"*Nunca,*" Marcos answered. "Other than Carlos, Antonio is my most trusted dive master." He shook his head in disappointment.

Señor Domínguez didn't say anything, but he kept glancing down at his watch willing the time to go slower. If Antonio didn't arrive in the next three minutes, he would have to call someone else to fill in for the missing dive guide.

"It's your call," *Señor Domínguez* said to the lead dive master after the time was up.

Marcus sighed and his lips sagged.

"I don't know. Let's wait one more minute." Marcos looked tormented because he knew if another dive guide had to be brought in, Antonio could very well lose his job, and he didn't want to lose another good dive guide after losing one already.

Chapter Thirty-One

With time running out before the morning boat had to leave, *señor Domínguez* could not wait for Antonio any longer, and he ended up calling someone to fill in for the missing dive guide. When everyone was finally on board, I watched the crew depart from the dock. I stood there lost in thought for a few minutes as the boat grew smaller and smaller as it headed south of the island. When I could no longer see the boat, I turned away to face Aiden.

"What should we do now?"

"I don't know," Aiden shrugged. "Why don't we get some coffee while we try to figure out what to do. I'm still a guest at the resort, so we can go the café."

"Coffee would be excellent, but what about Luna?" I said looking at the dog beside me.

"Let's ask Elena if she can keep an eye on her while we get coffee and something to eat. We can bring back some pastries for them after we're done."

"That sounds like a plan," I said.

Elena was in the backroom sorting through rental gear when

we entered the office. Luna went straight to the doghouse and laid down.

"Look at that! Luna's ready for a nap," I said and laughed at the little dog.

"*¡Hola,* Claire*! ¡Hola,* Aiden*!*

"*¡Hola* Elena*!* How are you this morning?"

"I'm good, but I'm worried about Antonio not showing up," Elena said as she picked up two mismatching fins.

"It's weird he didn't show up because we just saw him last night at dinner. He seemed distracted when he left," I recalled Antonio's odd behavior.

Elena stopped sorting equipment and looked at me. She looked troubled.

"Can I trust you guys with something?" Elena whispered. She looked over at the door to make sure that no one else was near.

"What is it?" Aiden asked.

Elena darted her eyes around the shop. She didn't see anyone inside other than Aiden and me. Elena whispered," well, I heard Antonio and *señor Domínguez* talking in the dive shop last night. I came back after I realized I forgot to set the alarm at the shop. There are thousands of dollars worth of scuba gear in the store."

We inched closer.

Lowering my voice, I inquired, "did you hear what they were talking about?"

"No, they were upstairs in *señor Domínguez's* office with the door shut, but I heard Antonio shout, "I don't have the money! I didn't stay after that because I didn't want *señor Domínguez* to think I was being nosy. Plus, I didn't want to get in trouble for not setting the alarm in the building. When I came in this morning, I thought he was going to chide me for leaving the shop unsecured, but *señor Domínguez* didn't even mention the alarm."

Elena seemed surprised by the two men's conversation, but it seemed as though she was more concerned that the owner didn't chastise her for not setting the alarm than Antonio's outburst.

I was disturbed by the receptionist's information, but there wasn't anything I could do.

"Elena, would you mind keeping an eye on Luna? Aiden and I are going to the café to get some breakfast and coffee. We can bring back something for you too."

"Sure, I'll watch Luna, but I don't think it'll be necessary because it looks like she is taking a nap in her house." Elena smiled at the sweet little dog.

"Thank you!" I called out as Aiden and I made our way out the door.

We strolled down the beach path back to the hotel area. We got to an area where there were some tall bushes and palm trees when I thought I heard someone call my name. I stopped to listen.

I heard a hoarse whisper. "Claire! It's me."

"Who's there?" I asked grabbing Aiden's arm.

The bushes opened to reveal Antonio hiding behind the thick leaves.

"What are you doing skulking in the dark, Antonio?" I asked in surprise. I crept closer to get a better look. He was wearing the same Scuba Mar polo shirt as yesterday.

"I was hoping to find you," Antonio explained still partially blocked by the thicket. "I was on the way to the hostel when I saw you talking to Marcos and *señor Domínguez.*"

"Why didn't you go to work? Everyone is looking for you." Aiden recounted to Antonio how the lead dive guide and the owner had been frantically looking for him.

"I know," Antonio said looking scared.

"So why are you hiding, and why did you want to find me?" I asked again still mystified why Antonio was acting so strange.

"I need your help." The five o'clock shadow stood out on his pale face. Antonio licked his lips nervously and blurted out, "I'm being blackmailed by *señor Domínguez*."

"What!" Aiden and I were astounded by what we had heard. Antonio may have just told us he was being chased by aliens and that was why he was hiding in the bushes.

"Why is *señor Domínguez* blackmailing you?" I questioned Antonio to get more clarity on the bizarre situation.

"I didn't tell you and Aiden last night, but I heard *señor* Drew and Carlos have their argument, and it made me mad that not only did *señor* Drew not show up for the *cenote* tour he asked me to set up, but he didn't leave a tip for Carlos. I didn't want *señor* Drew to think he could get away with treating people poorly," Antonio said.

"That seems reasonable," I said, but I was still baffled why he was being blackmailed by the owner of the dive shop. I was about to ask Antonio again to explain how the two things were related when he continued with his story.

"*Señor Domínguez* heard me talk to *señor* Drew, and he also saw me push him. I didn't mean to push him, but *señor* Drew was trying to get off the boat so he could get away from me. To prevent him from leaving, I pushed him back on the boat, and he fell backwards and hit his head. I didn't think I pushed him hard. It was an accident," Antonio cried in anguish and covered his eyes with his palms.

"Was Drew conscious after he hit his head?" I asked breathlessly.

"He was, but I didn't have my phone, so I ran to the office to call an ambulance because there was some blood on his head. When I came back a few minutes later to check on *señor* Drew again, he wasn't breathing. I thought he died because of me, so I panicked and left the area before anyone could see me," Antonio said as he hung his head in shame.

"If you left because you thought you killed Drew, why did you come back to work the next day?" The story was getting more outrageous. I looked at Aiden, and he was just as confused as I was.

"At first, I had no intention of coming back to work. In fact, I was at my apartment debating whether I should pack my bags and leave for Cancun or wait to see if the police would knock on my door. I guess I was still dazed from what happened because I didn't move from the couch in my apartment. In fact, I fell asleep there. It wasn't until later in the evening when I woke up and the police didn't come to get me. I thought maybe Drew was not dead after all, and the whole thing was a dream."

"When I went to work the next day, *señor Domínguez* found me alone loading my gear on the boat and told me he saw me push Drew on the boat. He said I killed him when he hit his head, and he would call the police if I didn't give him 1,000,000 Mexican pesos." Antonio pounded his fist into his hand recounting what the dive owner threatened him with.

I couldn't believe what I was hearing. "*Señor Domínguez* wanted 1,000,000 pesos for not going to the police?" I mentally calculated how much that would be in dollars.

Aiden whistled as he also did the math. "That's about $50,000 US. I wonder why he wanted that much money."

"I don't know why he wanted that much, but it's a sum of money I don't have!" Antonio yelled. "It would take me years to make that kind of money as a diving guide, and *señor Domínguez* knew it would be impossible for me to come up with that kind of money in such a short amount of time."

I was sympathetic to what Antonio told me, but I was confused why Antonio continued to work that day as our guide. I was with him the entire day, and I had no idea anything was wrong. There was something going on that didn't make any sense to me.

I pinched the bridge of my nose. "I have a headache, and I need coffee," I moaned shaking my head.

Aiden put one hand on my lower back and patted it comfortingly.

I looked at Aiden, and he looked wary of what he just heard. The three of us stood motionless unsure of the next step. From a distance, I heard Luna barking.

With the need of caffeine growing stronger, I said, "let's go get some coffee and talk about this more." Aiden and I moved towards the resort, but Antonio remained rooted where he was.

Chapter Thirty-Two

"What's wrong Antonio?"

"I know it looks really bad Claire because I pretended I was not involved in anything," Antonio said sadly. "But you have to understand that everything was spinning out of control inside my head. I wanted to say something to you on the boat, but I couldn't get you alone without the others getting suspicious. Then at the restaurant, after I told you about how *señor* Drew left me responsible for paying for *cenote* trip, I thought you were suspicious I had something to do with his death.

"I'm really sorry Antonio. I'm struggling to comprehend what you just told me. Did you know Carlos was arrested for Drew's death when you went to work the next day? If so, why did you act so- well, normal?" I looked at him in befuddlement and continued. "If my friend was taken into custody for something I may have done, I would be distraught."

"I know," Antonio said. "I have no excuse."

I looked at Aiden to see what he thought. He looked back and me and shrugged his shoulders in bewilderment.

"Antonio, why didn't you say anything at the restaurant.

When you went on and on about the *cenote diving*, I didn't get a sense anything was troubling you," I said still not fully believing Antonio's confession.

"I know. I'm sorry! I didn't know how to talk to you separately at the restaurant to explain what happened, and after I remembered how *señor* Drew treated me, I got angry, so I left. Out of habit, I walked back to the dive shop and saw the light was on in *Señor Domínguez's* office."

"Did you know someone heard your conversation with *señor Domínguez*?" I left out Elena's name because I didn't want her to get into trouble.

"No. Who was it?"

Before I could come up with an excuse, Antonio shook his head and said, "I skipped work today to find you at your hostel. I was on the way to your place when I saw you talking to Marcos and *señor Domínguez*, so I decided to hide and wait until you left the dive shop area. I almost didn't call out your name because I wasn't sure if I could trust Aiden." Antonio said as he looked at Aiden to seek confirmation whether he could trust him or not.

Aiden nodded his head and said, "look, I don't know if you are telling Claire and me the entire truth, but I don't think you killed Drew. At least, not on purpose."

Antonio gulped but remained silent.

I felt torn over Antonio's confession. On the one hand, I wanted Antonio to go to the police and tell them what he had just told me and Aiden. On the other hand, if he told the police that he pushed Drew, the police might release Carlos and take Antonio into custody.

"What do we do?" I asked the guys.

As Aiden and I stood on the beach path, and Antonio remained hidden in the bushes, Aiden explained what we needed to do.

"Listen Antonio. I know you must be scared, but you have

to go to the police and tell them what you just told us. Carlos is locked up, and he is innocent," he said.

Antonio looked defeated, but he knew Aiden was right, so he said, "I will go to the police. Then he looked at me and said, "will you come with me?"

"Of course, we will!" I said for the both of us, but I looked at Aiden to see if he agreed. Since he was nodding his head, I took it as a sign of acceptance. "I'll tell the police it was an accident, and you didn't mean to harm Drew when you pushed him."

Like Aiden, I wasn't completely certain Antonio was telling us the whole truth but given the fact he hadn't fled the island led me to believe he was innocent. We still had to figure out why the owner of the dive shop wanted to blackmail Antonio, but in the meantime, we had to go to the police station so Antonio could tell Detective Martinez what happened and try to get Carlos out of jail.

"Thank you!" Antonio sighed in relief as he came out of the dark and onto the path. The three of us walked from the beach to the street where we could catch a taxi downtown to the police station. I flagged one of the numerous taxis driving along the street. Almost immediately a small, white, compact car pulled over to let Antonio and me talk to the driver from the passenger's side.

"*Sí-senorita*?" The taxi driver called out.

"We want to go downtown," I replied. When the driver motioned for us to come into the cab, Antonio opened the back passenger door to let Aiden and me go in first. Then Antonio shut the door and opened the front passenger door to sit beside the driver.

"Where to *amigos*? The driver asked as he turned the steering wheel to bring the car back on the road again.

"The metro police department," Antonio responded. The driver turned his head and looked at Antonio suspiciously and then looked at the rearview mirror at the passengers sitting in the back seat.

"My friend lost something valuable, and he wants to report the theft." I said trying to put the driver at ease.

The driver nodded at my explanation and said," Cozumel is a beautiful place with friendly people, but unfortunately, we do have some problems with petty crime. You must hide your belongings very carefully *señorita*, away from any windows." The driver continued to drone on about how much the crime rate in the area had gone up from when he was a kid growing up on the island. I nodded my head occasionally in agreement without really hearing what the driver said.

Before long, the taxi stopped at the guard gate, and the driver told the security guard his passengers wanted to report a theft to the police. The guard wrote something down on a piece of paper that was on a clip board. Then, he lifted the gate arm up so the taxi could continue to the station.

"Okay, we're here," the driver said as he pulled into the circular front driveway that led to the main doors.

"*Gracias*. How much?" I asked.

The driver replied, "30 Mexican pesos or $1.50 U.S."

I reached into my purse and pulled out my wallet. I took out several bills and handed them to the driver.

"*Gracias señorita*!" The driver said and smiled happily when he saw I had included a tip.

"*Gracias señor*. Have a good day." I said as I hurriedly got out of the car to catch up with Antonio who was walking resolutely towards the entrance. It seemed Antonio wanted to get things over with as quickly as possible. I hoped the detectives would consider it a positive step Antonio had come in on his own accord and to not take him into custody. But we would have to wait and see what happened after we met with Detective Martinez.

The same uniformed police officer was sitting at the front

desk typing on his keyboard when we walked into the station. He looked up from his computer to greet us. At first, he didn't recognize me, but his eyes lit up in familiarity when I told him my name. "Detective Rojas is not here, but would you like to speak to Detective Martinez?" The police officer asked.

"Yes, my friend and I would like to speak to the detective please," I said. At the word "friend," the police officer noticed Antonio standing next to me. He closely peered at Antonio who was still wearing his clothes from yesterday. With his rumpled clothes and disheveled hair, he looked sketchy.

"And you *señor*? Do you wish to talk to the detective as well?" The officer inquired as he glanced at Aiden who was hovering behind me.

"No, I'm just here to support my friends." Aiden answered. When Antonio heard Aiden say "friends," he smiled appreciatively at him.

"What's your name?" The officer asked as his attention went back to Antonio.

"*Antonio Rodriguez Flores*," Antonio said. The officer wrote down our names in the police log and then picked up the phone and paged Detective Martinez. He then pointed to some hard, orange plastic seats across his desk and said, "have a seat over there, and the detective will come to get you."

We walked over to the chairs, but neither one of us sat down. I was too anxious to talk to the detective while Antonio was a little scared. Instead, we paced back and forth around the room. Occasionally, Antonio would heave a big sigh and run his hand through his short, dark, curly hair making it stick out even more. Even though Antonio looked frazzled from all the worrying, he still reminded me of a Mexican *telenovela* actor. With his dark hair and tan skin, he was quite dashing. I had to remind myself this was not the time to check out someone, especially if he turned out to be a murderer.

Speaking of an attractive guy, I sneaked a glance at Aiden. It was crazy how Aiden ended up being involved in helping Antonio and me. I wondered if he was committed to helping Carlos or if he was there because he wanted to impress me. In either case, I was glad he was there.

A few minutes later, I saw the detective walking down the hall towards the waiting area. Today, Detective Martinez was wearing pumps with a two-inch heel with her normal pantsuit. I looked at my tank top and cutoff shorts and compared what I was wearing to the detective's clothes. I thought the detective looked sophisticated and wished I could look put together as the policewoman. However, the thought of myself wearing a pantsuit made me let out an untimely snort as I pictured myself playing dress up. Fortunately, no one heard me, and I was glad that they couldn't read my thoughts.

The detective stopped a few feet away from me and extended her hand. "*Señorita* O' Keefe, it is good to see you again." We shook hands briefly, and then the detective turned to Antonio and extended her hand to him and said, "*buenos dias. Yo soy la detective Martinez.*"

Antonio took the detective's hand and shook it. "*Buenos dias, me llamo Antonio.*"

"*Mucho gusto.*" Detective Martinez replied and turned to Aiden and greeted him as well before she turned back to Antonio.

"Officer Escobar said that you wanted to speak with me. What would you like to tell me?"

"Is there somewhere private that we can talk?" I asked as I discreetly gestured to the police officer sitting at the desk who was obviously listening to the conversation even though he had his eyes trained on the computer monitor.

The detective's eyes narrowed slightly as though she thought the three people in front of her were going to waste her time when she had a lot of important things to do. But her impeccable training forbade her from expressing those thoughts aloud, so she gave us a terse smile and said, "*claro que si*-of course."

She waved her hand for us follow her to her office, and then the detective walked in a quick clip. The three of us walked briskly to keep up with her. When we reached her office, the door was open, so Detective Martinez motioned with her head for us to go in first. Since there were only two chairs in front of her desk, Aiden gestured to me and Antonio that we should sit in the chairs, and he would remain standing. I thought to myself that Aiden was so thoughtful and not like so many other guys I had dated. He was considerate and that made him more attractive to me than he already was.

As Antonio and I sat down, the detective went around the desk and sat down in her office chair. This time the detective didn't bother to offer refreshments. It was too bad because I was sorely in need of caffeine. I would even be glad to drink the syrupy concoction the detective made for me last time.

"Well, what is it you want to tell me?" The detective asked, getting down to business. She folded her hands on the desk and made it apparent she didn't think either Antonio or I would have anything that would be of interest to her judging by the expression on her face.

Antonio glanced at me, and I gave him an encouraging nod. "I would like to give some information about the guest that died from our dive shop a few days ago. His name is Andrew Markle."

At the mention of the resort victim's name, Detective Martinez's eyes grew a little larger, but she remained silent and nodded her head to encourage Antonio to continue talking.

Ha! I thought. It appears now we do have information that is worth your time.

"On the day that *señor* Drew died, I had an argument with him after we came back from our dive," Antonio said quickly as he avoided looking directly at Detective Martinez. Instead, he looked at me hoping I would give him the confidence to tell the rest of the story.

I gave him a reassuring smile.

"What did you have the confrontation about?" The detective asked.

"I confronted *señor* Drew because I heard that he didn't leave a tip for the diving crew after the day's trip, and it made me mad because he didn't show up for a dive I set up for him previously. As a result, I got stuck paying for his trip because he didn't cancel his reservation."

"What dive trip are you talking about?" The detective inquired. "Was it through Scuba Mar?"

"No, in addition to working for Scuba Mar, I also set up dive tours to the *cenotes* in Tulum with a dive shop I know. Usually, the customer pays the dive shop directly, but the victim-*señor* Drew- told me that he didn't have his wallet with him when I called the shop and told me if I went ahead and paid for it, he would pay me back. He also mentioned he would include something extra with the payment he owed me. *Señor* Drew winked when he said this, so I expected to get a big tip from him and not to be let down," Antonio explained.

I could picture Drew's smug face when he implied he would leave Antonio a tip if he did him the favor of paying for his trip in advance. The thought of someone being so rude knowing the dive guides counted on the generosity of the tourist divers made me sick to my stomach. If he wasn't already dead, I would have given him an earful.

"What happened after you talked to the victim?" The detective pressed. She seemed impatient to get to the bottom of the story.

"While I was talking to him, he started to walk away, so I grabbed his arm. He tried to pull his arm away, but when he pulled away, he lost his footing and slipped. He must have hit his head hard on the deck of the boat because he passed out. I leaned down to see if he was still breathing, but when I saw some blood by his head, I left to call an ambulance."

"When you went to call for help, did you know the man was still alive?" The detective asked.

"Yes, I knew he was still alive because he was breathing," Antonio said. His tan skin had a whitish pallor as he recalled the details of his encounter with Drew. I was inclined to believe everything Antonio was saying, but it still didn't solve why the dive shop owner threatened to blackmail him. If he was truly innocent, Antonio would have been able to tell *señor Domínguez* that his threats held no power over him. As I was wrestling with this line of thought, I heard Detective Martinez continue to grill Antonio.

"Why didn't you report this earlier?"

"I was scared I would be taken away like Carlos?" Antonio explained.

The detective's eyes narrowed in disapproval, and she said, "that's right. Since no one saw you argue with the victim, but there were several people who saw Carlos argue with him, you let people assume it was Carlos's fault."

Antonio did not reply back because he knew what Detective Martinez said was true. He hung his head in shame.

"Why are you here *senorita*?" The detective asked as she turned her attention to me. I sat listening to Antonio without saying anything.

"She is here because I asked her to come with me," Antonio said quietly, still stinging from the detective's admonishment. "Aiden is also here to support me."

The detective frowned but acknowledged Antonio's explanation and saw there was nothing wrong with his friends there to support him.

Despite my reservations about Antonio, I felt bad for him and stepped in the conversation.

"What my friend didn't say was that he is being blackmailed

by the owner of the dive shop," I volunteered. "*Señor Domínguez* witnessed the argument between Antonio and Drew and saw when Drew fell and hit his head. He told Antonio he needed to pay him $1,000,000 Mexican pesos, or he would go to the police." I told the astounded detective.

With this new piece of information, Detective Martinez became silent to digest what she just heard. At the beginning of Antonio's confession, it seemed he was the reason the American died. However, the fact that the victim was still alive when the dive guide went to get help and the part about being black-mailed shed a different light on the events that happened. The detective made a steeple with her hands and rested her chin on them but didn't say anything. She continued to stare at us trying to determine if we were lying about the events of Drew's death.

"The fact that the owner of the dive shop didn't tell you this information should make the police suspicious. I highly recommend interviewing *señor Domínguez* again." Aiden added from where he stood behind Claire and Antonio. He had been quiet until now.

When the detective gave a hard look at Aiden, he explained he was a criminal attorney in the United States. Although Antonio had not retained his services, he would be happy to volunteer as his counsel if he needed it.

Antonio was overwhelmed by Aiden's support, and he jumped out of the chair to give him a big hug.

"Thank you so much *amigo*!" he cried in gratitude.

"You're welcome." Aiden hugged him back, but he was caught off-guard by Antonio's sudden gesture of affection.

Man! I thought. Aiden's stock is really going up in my view.

"In light of what you told me, I must speak with the owner of the dive shop." Detective Martinez said as she pursed her lips together. Then she picked up her phone to send police officers to bring in the dive shop owner for questioning. After she made her request, she placed the phone receiver down and told us we needed to wait in the lobby until she received more information.

Before we left the detective's office, I remembered to ask, "what about Carlos? Are you going to let him go?"

The detective paused for a moment but then she answered, "since your friend admitted he was the last person to speak with the victim, we can assume Carlos wasn't involved with Andrew Markle's death. However, until we determine exactly how and when the victim died, your friend needs to be available for further questioning."

"What about me," Antonio asked. He looked very nervous at what the detective might say next. "You claimed the man was still breathing when you called for help, and we cannot tell for certain if it was your push that caused the victim to die," the detective mused. "However, we don't know for certain if the fall didn't cause his death even if it was an accident, so I must ask you to stay here at the precinct until we are able to review all the information we just heard."

"Do you need to take me into custody?" Antonio pressed.

The detective stood up and sighed, "No, not yet." She went to the door and opened it. We said our thanks and walked out.

"That went better than I thought it would," I said looking at Aiden and Antonio. "At least they didn't take you into custody."

"Not yet." Antonio licked his lips.

"It's a good sign they didn't take you, and they are going to release Carlos." Aiden chimed in. Aiden's authority as a lawyer helped put Antonio at ease, and as we walked back towards the waiting area, we felt a little lighter compared to how we felt when we first entered the police building.

Chapter Thirty-Three

Aiden, Antonio, and I went back to the sitting area and sat down silently waiting to see what would happen. I focused my gaze on the clock that was hung on a wall in front of me ticking the seconds away. I was lost in thought thinking about Drew's death, so I was startled when my phone buzzed from my travel purse. As usual, I had a difficult time locating it in my messy bag, but I finally grabbed it before the buzzing stopped. I looked at the name of the caller and smiled when I saw it was Julia.

"Hey!" I said in greeting. I stood up to walk a few steps away from the guys, so I could have more privacy talking to my friend.

"Hey yourself!" Julia replied. "Have you solved who killed Drew and got your friend out of jail?"

"No to the first question but maybe to the second," I said. Aware I was in a public place, I didn't want to provide any details that someone could overhear. "How's the wedding planning going?" I asked Julia to change the subject. My friend picked up the clue and changed the topic without missing a beat.

"It's alright, but I'm worried you may not get to San Francisco in time for the rehearsal dinner. You are supposed to be my maid of honor and give a speech at the reception." Julia said this evenly, but I knew she was concerned something might happen. If we were talking on FaceTime, I would be able to see her worried expression.

"Yes, yes, I know, and I promise I will be there. In fact, I'm leaving Cozumel tomorrow for San Fran." I assured Julia, but secretly, I wondered if I would be able to find out who had committed the crime before I was scheduled to depart the island. Even though my initial plan was to free Carlos from jail, I now also wanted to solve Drew's death.

To my friends and family's dismay, I was naturally curious and doing detective work suited my personality, sometimes it distracted me from doing what I was supposed to be doing. That's probably why Julia called. She wanted to check on me because she remembered all the times from our college days when we made plans, I would veer from them because something caught my attention.

"Don't worry, I'll be there." I reassured Julia. "And you don't have to pick me up from the airport. I'll catch an Uber to your apartment. Tell Grumpy to get ready to be spoiled by auntie Claire." Although I wanted to give more information to my friend including the fact Aiden was here helping me, I was worried telling Julia would raise more questions I couldn't elaborate more on the details.

Julia let out a big sigh knowing this was all the information she was going to get from me.

"Be careful Claire!" Julia warned me.

"Yes, mom," I teased. I heard Julia chuckle as she ended the call.

I was putting the phone back into my purse when I spotted Carlos walking our way.

"Carlos!" I cried out excitedly. Hearing me speak out, Antonio looked to where his coworker was and waved when he saw Carlos coming towards us. We could see Carlos was wearing the same Scuba Mar polo shirt Antonio had on and some khaki shorts. He didn't look too rough, so I assumed the police gave him something else to wear during his confinement and let him take showers.

Carlos gave me a big hug and said, "*gracias amiga*!" The detectives told me you stopped by to see how I was doing. Thank you so much for caring and being my friend. Yup, I thought, as I hugged my friend back. Carlos smelled of a woodsy soap rather than a body odor that would have been evident if his attendants had not let him use the showering facilities. Why these thoughts flowed through my head at this moment was beyond me. Along with being curious, thinking random thoughts was also a trait of mine that usually annoyed my friends and family.

After he greeted me, Carlos turned Antonio and Aiden. "*Hola amigos*!" Are you guys here to see me too? Wow, I'm so lucky to have such good friends." Carlos grinned and kept looking back and forth from me to Aiden, and Antonio. While Aiden and I were genuinely happy to see Carlos released from jail, Antonio looked uncomfortable and said, "well, I don't know how you will feel after I tell you why I came here, but you should know the truth." Carlos' happiness faded, but he let Antonio explain. With my help, Antonio quickly told Carlos what happened between him and Drew.

At first, Carlos was bewildered by what he heard, but then he looked upset. However, he didn't look angry, and when Antonio finished talking, he reached out to his friend and said, "don't worry, I'm not mad at you."

"You're not?" asked Antonio. "Why not?" His mouth was agape in shock.

"I guess I would have done the same thing as you did," replied Carlos honestly.

"What!" We said at the same time.

"I think you already knew *señor* Drew did not leave me a

tip for that day's dive. However, the whole truth was that *señor* Drew did not tip me for the entire time he dove with the company. He told me on the first day he usually tips everyone including the dive masters on his last day. And he winked when he said that, so I thought I would get a pretty nice tip at the end. Instead, when I asked him politely if he had forgotten something, *señor* Drew pretended he didn't know what I was talking about and walked away. I followed him and told him it was customary for divers to leave a gratuity for their diving guides. Instead of apologizing, *señor* Drew looked at me and said he wasn't going to leave a tip for me or anyone else because he didn't think we did a good job taking care of him during his time with the company. He also said the diving guides spent way too much time paying attention to the other guests and didn't accommodate his wishes," said Carlos.

Carlos' description of what happened between him and Drew angered me. Uncharitably, I wished I could have hit him with an air tank for being such a jerk! There were some people who didn't leave tips because they were new to diving and didn't know the tipping etiquette. And there were also some people who gave small tips because they were stingy or couldn't afford a bigger gratuity. But I never heard of someone completely stiffing the crew over multiple days of diving. That was unheard of in the diving community.

I was still reeling in anger over what Carlos had told us I momentarily forgot Antonio was still looking for redemption from his co-worker.

"You're really not furious at me for not telling the police I was the one who pushed *señor* Drew and made him hit his head," Antonio inquired.

"No, I really am not." Carlos smiled at his friend.

Carlos' sympathetic admission made Antonio sag with relief. He gave his friend a big hug and thanked him. "I thought you would be angry with me for letting you take the blame for the American's death."

"I didn't like being in jail, but I was mostly confused because I didn't think my conversation with *señor* Drew had the power to kill him," said Carlos. "Then as the days went by without any new information, I grew upset." Seeing Antonio's expression, Carlos quickly added. "Like I said, I'm not angry at you, and I understood why you didn't want to report your argument with *señor* Drew. I just wished someone would have given me information about what was going on."

Aiden, being the observant and detailed lawyer, brought up a crucial detail Antonio forgot to mention while he tried to make amends with his friend. "Did you know *señor Domínguez* tried to blackmail Antonio?"

Carlos looked confused at Aiden's question. "I'm sorry... did you say *señor Domínguez* tried to blackmail you?"

"Oh yeah, I forgot to tell you. *Señor Domínguez* saw me talking to Drew, and he claimed the man died while I went to call for help after I pushed him," Antonio explained.

"*Señor Domínguez* told Antonio he needed to pay him $1,000,000 pesos, or he would go to the police and tell them that Antonio killed Drew," I added.

Carlos jerked his head back when he heard the amount.

"What did you do?" Carlos asked his friend.

"I didn't do or say anything because I was frightened. *Señor Domínguez* told me I had two days to bring him the money. Otherwise, he would go to the authorities," Antonio answered.

"Did you tell him you would give him the money?" Carlos asked.

"No! I don't have that kind of cash," Antonio exclaimed. I left the dive shop after *señor Domínguez* threatened me thinking I would have to leave Cozumel, but before I did, I ended taking a nap when I got home because I was so tired. When I woke up, I hoped that the whole thing was a bad dream."

"Why didn't you go to the police yourself?" Carlos pressed his friend still confused by what he heard.

"Honestly, I didn't know what to do. I went to work the next morning, and I was trying to get Claire by herself, so I could get her advice on what I should do. Even though I didn't know her very well, she seemed like a nice person, and when I heard her asking about you, I thought she might want to help me too," Antonio said.

My face flushed hearing Antonio say he thought I was a nice person. Aiden saw my reaction and squeezed my hand.

"I'm completely shocked *señor Domínguez* tried to blackmail you! I didn't think he would be the type of person that would ever do that. He always treated me kindly." Carlos said as he thought back to his former boss.

"*Señor Domínguez* always treated me well too which is why I thought I really did kill *señor* Drew because I didn't think he would lie about something like that," Antonio said.

"The question is why did he try to blackmail Antonio. If he really cared about him, why wouldn't he just tell Antonio without asking him to pay all that money?" I asked as the four of us fell into silence.

The sound of a text message being delivered on a phone broke us out of our revelry. Both Aiden and I looked at our phones to see whose phone got the text. When Aiden realized it was his phone, he clicked on the message to read the note from Ryan.

"Oh my gosh! I completely forgot Ryan and I arranged for a jeep tour around the island. He said we are leaving in an hour and, he is wondering where I am. Should I cancel?" Aiden looked apologetic.

"That's okay *amigo*, "Carlos said. "You should go with your friend on the tour. I don't think we can do anything at the moment."

"I think it's important we don't do anything out of the ordinary. Since Ryan doesn't know what's going on with Carlos or Antonio, we should keep things as normal as we can," I added.

Aiden nodded in agreement, but he seemed hesitant about going. I thought he might be reluctant to leave me, but I didn't want to voice that aloud.

"Alright, I'll go, but if you guys need me, don't hesitate to text," Aiden said glancing at me as he said this.

"Thank you for coming with me to the station," Antonio said as he hugged Aiden. Then, Carlos reached out to shake hands with Aiden. When Aiden turned to me, he bent down to give me a hug, and he whispered in my ear so the other two guys couldn't hear. "If you feel unsafe at any time, shoot me a text." With that, he smiled at me and turned to leave the police station.

Chapter Thirty-Four

A few hours later, two burly police officers burst into the station and strutted past Antonio, Carlos, and me while we waited for Detective Martinez to tell us that we could leave. When one of the officers rapped on the detective's door, a muffled voice told them to enter. Both officers went into the room and out of sight.

I wondered what they were telling the detective, but I didn't have much time to ponder because the door opened, and Detective Martinez and the two officers trailing behind her marched over to where my friends and I were standing.

"The officers could not find *señor Domínguez*. It seems he has fled his dive shop. The receptionist said she saw him leave his office shortly after the morning dive boat left the pier, but she didn't know where he was going. She had no reason to think that he could be abandoning his business for good or that anything was wrong, so she didn't call the police after he left," Detective Martinez said solemnly when she reached the waiting area.

We exchanged dismayed looks but said nothing.

"Do you think he left the island?" I asked finally.

"We don't know," the detective replied. She pursed her lips. Her eyes bored into us, and it was unnerving to have her stare at us like that.

I was devastated that *señor Domínguez* may have disappeared, but the reality was none of us knew for sure. In fact, we didn't even know why *señor Domínguez* was trying to blackmail Antonio.

"Do you know where he lived?" One of the uniformed police officers asked hoping to get additional information.

"No," we replied.

"*Señor Domínguez* was very friendly with the staff and the guests, but he was a private person. No one knew what he did when he was not at work." Carlos added.

"Now that you mention it, no one knew if he was married or had kids," said Antonio. The lack of information about the dive shop owner surprised me because most Mexicans I knew were very open about their lives. Then I became depressed thinking about the lack of evidence that would lead us to the real murderer.

I also found it puzzling the owner operated a scuba diving shop and school but didn't know how to dive. This tidbit of gossip was something I found out from Carlos on our first day of diving together. I remembered this detail because I joked to Carlos that maybe I should open a scuba diving shop instead of teaching, so I could dive anytime I wanted to.

At the time, Carlos laughed, but he told me not all scuba diving operations were owned by scuba divers. Carlos mentioned the owner of Scuba Mar bought the school and diving operation because the previous owner mismanaged it so badly he had to sell it. *Señor Domínguez* bought the company for a steal, and when he partnered with the resort, he made even more money off his venture.

"Do we need to continue to stay here, or can we leave?" Carlos asked Detective Martinez.

"You may leave, but please leave your contact information with the police officer at the reception desk, so we know how to get ahold of you if we have more questions," answered Detective Martinez as she looked down at her wristwatch.

We agreed we would leave our personal information with the police officer, and afterwards, we walked out of the building and stood breathing the salty air.

Taking a deep breath Antonio asked, "so, what do we do now?"

"I know this might be a bad time to get something to eat, but are you guys hungry? I have had nothing but jail food for the past few days, and I would love to eat something fresh," said Carlos.

"Why don't we go back to the restaurant where we had those lionfish tacos," Antonio chimed in.

"You mean, *La Café de Marisco?*" asked Carlos.

"*Sí*!" Antonio responded. "Do you know the restaurant?"

"Yes, I have never been there, but I passed it several times because it's close to Scuba Mar," Carlos replied.

"That's a great idea." I said as I hailed a taxi that was parked close to the police station.

The driver saw me waving my arm and drove over to us. He got out of the driver's side to open the passenger door.

"*Hola amigos*! Where do you want to go?" The driver asked with a friendly smile.

"*Hola señor*! Can you take us the *La Café de Marisco*?" I asked the driver.

"Of course!" The taxi driver replied. The ride to the restaurant didn't take long, and the three of us sat in silence lost in our own thoughts.

"Okay, this is it." The driver said as he stopped in front of the small beachfront restaurant.

As I reached for my purse, Antonio motioned to us he would pick up the fare. I guessed he still felt guilty for letting Carlos take the blame for Drew's death. We scooted out of the cab and walked to the restaurant. By this time, my stomach was growling loudly. I was glad the music from inside the restaurant and the noise from the street masked the rumbling sounds that were coming from my digestive system.

The hostess remembered Antonio and me from the day before and led us to a table on the back patio. With the food and drinks ordered, we sat watching the waves roll on the beach. With many of the tourists gone from the winter high season, the beaches were mostly empty. During the high tourist season, it was hard to spot the white sand from all the towels and chairs that dotted the beach. Now, I could see miles and miles of pure white sand. As I stared out at the waves and thought about how thankful I was Antonio and I had found a way to get Carlos released from jail. However, I was disappointed we didn't find out who had killed Drew. I knew I had to leave tomorrow, but I really wanted to find out what had happened.

I looked away from the water to my friends. "How do you think Drew died?" I directed my question at Antonio. "You mentioned he was still breathing when you went to call the ambulance, but somehow between the time you left him and came back, he stopped breathing."

Antonio was eating some tortilla chips, but he paused in the middle of putting a chip with salsa in his mouth. He swallowed what he was eating and shrugged. "I really don't know Claire. He was still breathing, and although there was some blood, it didn't look like there was much, which was why I felt it was okay to leave him and get help. I didn't think he was in danger of dying."

"That meant either Drew was in more serious condition than you thought, or someone else came by while you were gone and did something to him," I said puzzled by what happened.

"Do you think *señor Domínguez* went to *señor* Drew when you left and killed him?" Carlos asked.

"I don't know," Antonio said. "I don't know why he would want to hurt *señor* Drew."

"Maybe he wanted to kill Drew and blame you so then he could blackmail you," I said.

"Why would he even want to blackmail Antonio or anyone in the first place," Carlos wondered aloud.

There were so many questions, and the three of us didn't have any answers. At the beginning, I wasn't sure if Antonio had anything to do with Drew's murder, but it didn't seem like he had a motive. Actually, I thought, he did have a motive, but I wasn't sure that not leaving someone a tip would make someone angry enough to want to kill a person.

The lionfish tacos arrived, and we devoured the food. They were just as good as they were the day before. I was glad the lion-fish was not native to the waters of Cozumel so divers could go out there and catch these fish to eat and help the local environment at the same time. While we were finishing the last of our drinks, Antonio spotted someone in the distance.

"Hey, isn't that *señor Domínguez*?"

"What?" Carlos and I said at the same time. I leaned forward to see where Antonio was pointing at.

"Look, over there! There is a man trying to get on a boat that is docked by the pier." Antonio said as he pointed in the direc-tion of the resort's pier that was used by the scuba diving guests.

"Yes, I think you are right!" Carlos said. This time, I could see there was a man by the boat, but he was too far away for me to tell if it was the dive shop owner. There was only one way to confirm it was the same person that we and the police were looking for.

"You guys need to get over there to see if it's *señor Domínguez* and make sure he doesn't leave on the boat. I'm going to pay for the food and call Detective Martinez," I said to my friends.

Antonio and Carlos nodded in agreement and stood from the table. Thankfully, the back patio was right beside the beach, so it wouldn't take long for the guys to get to the pier. While the guys jogged over to confront *señor Domínguez*, I went to the front of the restaurant with my wallet already in my hand.

"How was every-"

"It was very delicious! I'm sorry to be rude, but there is an emergency, and I want to pay for the food and leave immediately," I explained apologetically.

The hostess looked a little taken back, but she said, "Of course, I understand. The dinner is 300 pesos. I hope everything was good." The hostess said unsure if we were abruptly leaving because we didn't like the food, or if something was truly wrong.

"Everything was delicious!" I said, and I handed over some bills.

"Gracias!" The hostess smiled in relief.

After I paid the bill, I exchanged the wallet for the phone in my purse. Fortunately, as I was taking out the phone, I managed to snag Detective Martinez's business card with it. In my nervousness, my fingers shook, so I had to press the numbers several times, but I finally pushed the send button on the screen.

On the second ring, I heard Detective Martinez answer, *"bueno!"*

"Detective Martinez, this is Claire O'Keefe. My friend Antonio spotted *señor Domínguez* by the resort pier. He looks like he is trying to leave the area by boat. Please come right away."

"You said *señor Domínguez* is by the resort pier. Are you talking about the dock that Scuba Mar uses to load the guests and equipment?" Detective Martinez asked me for confirmation.

"Yes, that's it. Antonio and Carlos are heading to the pier

right now to prevent *señor Domínguez* from leaving," I answered.

"Please stay where you are and don't try to go after your friends. We don't know if *señor Domínguez* is dangerous, but he may be desperate and do something if you and your friends block his escape. We will be there as soon as we can. Keep your phone close to you," Detective Martinez told me and ended the call.

Chapter Thirty-Five

E ven though Detective Martinez warned me to stay put because *señor Domínguez* could be dangerous, my curiosity got the better of me. Besides, I wanted to watch over my friends who just went out of sight, and I wanted to be ready to call for help if I saw they were in trouble. Trying to act casually, like a tourist enjoying an afternoon on the beach, I strolled closer to the resort pier.

When I was about fifty feet from the pier, I realized I couldn't spot Antonio or Carlos and more worryingly, I did not see the dive shop owner anywhere. As I wandered along the sandy beach, I hoped my friends were not in distress, and *señor Domínguez* had not already fled the area. I debated for a few seconds whether I should go closer when I saw *señor Domínguez* come up from below the deck of the boat with a gun in his hand. The dive shop owner looked furtively around the area. Fearing my friends might be in danger, I jogged towards the boat abandoning any pretense I was a beachgoer lapping up the sun and the sand.

The detective's warning rang in my head as I called out to

the dive shop owner when I saw that he was getting ready to take the boat from the pier.

"*Hola señor*!" I shouted and gave him a friendly wave. My heart was pounding very fast, and I could feel the blood pulsing in my head. *Oh, I really hope I don't pass out from nervousness,* I thought as I felt my throat tighten.

The dive shop owner looked surprised when he saw me walking toward him, but he calmly said, "*ah señorita, hola.* I hope you are enjoying this beautiful day." He said the words casually in his deep and melodic voice, but his shifty looks gave his intention away, and I could tell that he was anxious to leave the area.

"*Sí*, with many of the tourists gone for the season, it's nice to have the beaches empty," I replied while thinking to myself, where is the police? The pounding in my head got louder. Since I was in college, I started practicing yoga and learned meditative breathing. Breathing through my nose with my mouth closed, I tried to slow my racing heart as I continued to apply the breathing technique that I learned from my instructors. I took a few more breaths, but they did nothing to relax me.

Señor Domínguez nodded his head briefly in acknowledgment and said, "yes, we had a very nice winter tourist season, and now that the day's diving trips are over, I'm going to take the boat on a relaxing sunset cruise."

Yeah, right I thought to myself- nice and relaxing with a gun. Where were Antonio and Carlos? I casually looked around trying to see if I could spot something that would lead me to their whereabouts. I was getting more worried as the time passed by, and the police still hadn't arrived. *Señor Domínguez* looked impatient to leave, so I stalled for more time.

"Um, may I use the bathroom?" I asked and pointedly looked at the boat's door that led below the deck. Using the bathroom was the first thing I could think of, and it wasn't completely inappropriate as the bathroom on the boat was probably the closest facility near the pier.

"*Uh, Sí,*" *señor Domínguez* said reluctantly after a few beats. I could tell he didn't want to let me on the boat, but there was no polite way of saying no without giving an elaborate excuse. I looked at him, and his mouth was pressed in a thin line.

"You can climb in over on that side." *Señor Domínguez* pointed to the back of the boat. I walked over and started to get in. With no one onboard to steady me as I climbed over the side, I almost slipped. To brace myself from falling, I put both hands on the deck in front of me. Because I was looking down at my hands, I didn't see the dive shop owner approach me. I became aware how close he was when he casted a shadow over me.

"Please be careful. You don't want to fall and hit your head," *señor Domínguez* said softly but forcefully. At those words, I brought up my head sharply and looked at him. I realized he used the same words to describe Drew's head injury. I looked at him in the eyes and a mutual understanding passed between us. In an instant, his demeanor had changed, and he had a hard look on his face, and worse, he lifted the gun from inside his shirt. With his back against the beach, it was impossible for a passerby to see the gun that was now pointed at me because the dive shop owner held it closely to his belly. With a jerk of his head, he motioned to me I should go down below the deck. Trying to maintain my balance on the wobbly boat, I carefully walked to the door that led below the deck.

When I reached the entry, I saw it was dark inside. The light was not turned on, so I had to let my eyes adjust to the dim lighting for a few seconds. When my eyes got acclimated to the dark, I looked around, and I saw a large lump on the floor against the back wall.

I heard the dive shop owner come down behind me, and he nudged me towards the big lump. As I got closer, I saw the lump was actually Antonio and Carlos tied closely together with their mouths gagged. I saw their eyes widen in disbelief when they saw me being pushed towards them.

"What did you do to my friends?" I shouted angrily.

"Your *amigos* tried to stop me from leaving. At first, they pretended to be friendly like you did. But then, they started to ask questions why I blackmailed Antonio and let Carlos take the blame for the American diver's death." *Señor Domínguez* talked rapidly as he moved closer to me.

"If your friends had not interfered in my leaving, then you would not be in this situation. And now they are going to die in the sea along with you!" *Señor Domínguez* spat out. "I don't want to harm the three of you, but I don't plan on being caught by the police." He pushed me so I fell on the floor close to my friends but not close enough where I could reach them.

"Wrap this rope around your feet three times tightly and then knot the ends." *Señor Domínguez* threw some nylon rope that the crew used to tie the buoys on the side of the boat to prevent it from being scratched when it was pier side.

I caught the rope with one hand and did as I was told, but I took my time. *Where was the police?* I thought frantically. I moved too slowly for *señor Dominguez's* liking, so he pointed the gun at me and said, "forget it! Hold out your hands together."

I held out my hands as *señor Domínguez* tucked the gun in the waist of his pants. He snatched the rope from me and wound the nylon so tight that I felt the circulation being cut from my wrists. Once he tied the rope around my hands, he pushed me back until I fell on my bottom. He grabbed my ankles to tie them together.

As the dive shop owner was binding my ankles together, I wondered if I could use my hands to punch *señor Domínguez* in the face and knock him out. It was a desperate idea, but I thought I could probably do it because I had a lot of upper body strength from all the years I spent swimming. This was one of the few times I was glad that I was not slender like Julia. Just as I was going to swing my hands at my captor, a shadow appeared at the entryway of the boat hatch.

I sighed as I made the shape of Detective Rojas standing at the opening with a gun pointed at *señor Domínguez*. I was overwhelmed with relief I didn't have to go through with my crazy plan, and I lowered my hands.

"Stop what you are doing right now. This is the police!" I heard the detective shout. "*Señor*, slowly raise your hands in the air!" the detective added firmly and loudly.

Señor Domínguez dropped my legs and raised his hands as he was told. He looked at me resignedly because he knew that he was not going to escape. Detective Rojas walked over to *señor Domínguez* and put a set of handcuffs on him. With the dive shop owner's hands cuffed behind him, the detective pulled the man up and walked him back to the opening. The police detective was so intent on taking the dive shop owner into custody that he temporarily forgot about me and my friends.

"What about us?" I piped up before the detective pushed my captor through the opening.

Detective Rojas stopped in his tracks by the sound of my voice. He looked at me and then replied, "I'll send someone down to untie you," he said as he pushed *señor Domínguez* into the open air and continued to take the wanted man back to his partner for questioning.

Since my captor didn't finish tying up my legs, I shook off the rope and walked over to where Antonio and Carlos were tied together. I took the gags out of their mouths so they could talk.

"*Gracias* Claire!" they said in unison.

"What happened? How did *señor Domínguez* end up tying you up together?" I asked my friends.

"Please untie our hands, and we'll fill you in on what happened," said Antonio.

As I worked to free their hands, Antonio told me they confronted *señor Domínguez* about Drew's death, and the dive shop owner admitted the American was still alive when Antonio left to call for the ambulance. However, when *señor Domínguez* went closer to inspect the diver, the man stopped breathing.

"So, *señor Domínguez* didn't kill Drew?" I asked. If the dive shop owner didn't kill Drew, why did he feel the need to blackmail Antonio and let Carlos take the blame. The entire thing was so perplexing.

"Well, it turned out that *señor Domínguez* had a gambling problem, and he owed someone who was very dangerous a lot of money, so he seized the opportunity to extort me for the money for Drew's death. Carlos was just an unfortunate victim in the whole scheme." Antonio relayed to me was he was told by his boss. "I have no idea why he told us this information unless he knew that he was going to kill us, so he didn't have to worry if he confessed his crime," Antonio added.

I was astounded by what I just heard. I had no idea that *señor Domínguez* was such a conniving person. "Did he say why he was running away?" I asked because I was still confused.

"Once Antonio disappeared this morning, *señor Domínguez* assumed Antonio was not going to pay the money he needed to pay off his gambling debt, so he fled shortly after the crew left for the morning dives, so no one knew he disappeared until the divers came back," Carlos said.

"Ah, I see," I said. Actually, I didn't, and I was dumbfounded by the story my friends were telling me. It seemed as though *señor Domínguez* went through a lot of trouble making an accidental death worse than it was. But until I heard the dive store owner's side of the story, nothing about what he did made sense to me. I was going to ask more questions to Carlos and Antonio, but then I saw Detective Martinez at the hatch.

"Are you okay? Do you need help freeing yourselves?" the detective asked the questions, but she could see that we didn't need help because we were standing without being bound by the rope.

"No, we are okay." I responded for the three of us. "How did you find us? How did you know that we were in this boat?"

"We figured this was the boat you told me on the phone because it was the only one on the pier. And there was a little dog that was barking madly outside near the it," Detective Martinez explained.

"A little dog?" I asked.

"Yes, there was a little brown and white dog. It looked like a chihuahua," the detective added.

"Luna!" Carlos and I said together.

"You know who Luna is?" Carlos turned to ask me.

"Yes, Elena and I have been taking care of her while you were in the police custody," I explained.

"Uh-hem!" Detective Martinez cleared her throat impatiently. She wasn't interested in our conversation about Luna.

"Sorry!" I said apologizing for being sidetracked.

The detective nodded and said, "then please come to the end of the dock as we have some questions to ask you." As detective Martinez stepped away from the opening, I thought to myself, *Yes, we also have some questions for you too.*

Chapter Thirty-Six

My friends and I followed Detective Martínez off the boat to the end of the pier where Detective Rojas stood waiting for us.

"You disobeyed our order to stay put," admonished Detective Rojas.

I knew I was guilty of not following orders, but I said defensively, "I didn't plan on confronting *señor Domínguez*. However, when I saw him go up to the bridge to take the boat from the pier, and I didn't see my friends, I made a decision to stop him."

Although the detective didn't like what he heard, my logic seemed to make sense. If I hadn't rushed to intervene, the dive shop owner might have taken the boat out to sea with Antonio and Carlos onboard.

"What's going to happen to *señor Domínguez*?" Antonio asked the question that was forefront on my mind.

"We are still trying to get all the details, but since he forcefully tied and threatened you with a gun, we will charge him with those actions for now," said the detective.

"Did *señor Domínguez* tell you why he wanted to harm you?" asked Detective Martinez.

"Yes!"

The two detectives looked stunned because they were not expecting an answer to this question.

"Go on," prodded Detective Martinez as she gave Antonio a look that said she was doubtful he could have a rational reason for the dive shop owner's bizarre behavior.

Antonio inhaled and let out a deep breath. Then, he proceeded to tell the detectives what he told me when we were on the boat. The detectives listened intently until he finished recounting what had happened.

"Let me get this straight," said the detective shaking his head in disbelief. "*Señor Domínguez* didn't kill the American diver, but he let everyone think Carlos killed him while at the same time tried to blackmail you for thinking you killed him? That makes no sense!" The two detectives looked at each other in amazement at the story they just heard.

Exactly my thought! I said silently.

"No, it doesn't, but I can imagine *señor Domínguez* wasn't thinking clearly as he had someone coming after him for the money he owed from gambling," said Carlos.

"As bizarre as *señor Domínguez*'s actions were, the real question is if *señor Domínguez* didn't kill Drew and neither did Antonio and Carlos, how did Drew die?" I asked the million-dollar question that no one had an answer to.

The sun began to set as the police questioned my friends and I, but they finally let us go for the evening. With nothing else to be done but wait for the information from the police after they questioned *señor Domínguez*, I told my friends I was going back to my hostel. I was mentally exhausted from the day's events, and I felt hot and sweaty from being out in the sun. All I wanted to do was take a nice and relaxing hot shower. I gave my friends a hug before I turned to walk down the path to my hostel.

Before I left, I told Carlos I had been bringing Luna home with me at the end of the day.

"Thank you so much for taking care of Luna. I really appreciate it, but I'll take her home with me tonight. Also, I will come tomorrow to go with you to the airport." Carlos said and gave me a kiss on both cheeks.

"That sounds great! Give Luna a big hug and lots of kisses on the nose. I'll see you tomorrow," I said and turned to give Antonio a hug.

Antonio hugged me back and kissed both of my cheeks too. "Bye, Claire! Thank you so much for believing me and coming with me to the police station. I really hope to see you again soon."

"I hope so too, and I hope you have a great time on the *cenote* tour tomorrow with Aiden, Ryan, and Peyton." I said and gave them one last wave.

After taking a leisurely shower, I sat on the bed and took out a book from my carry-on case. I always have a book with me, but I didn't get much of a chance to read on this trip because I was either diving or hanging out with my friends. However, I looked forward to putting aside the memory of the weird events that happened this evening by reading from a new series I discovered through one of my Instagram friends. Before I could get into the book, my phone played a K-pop song. At first I didn't recognize the number that was displayed on the screen, but then I thought it might be Aiden based off the 650 area code.

"Hello?" I spoke into my phone.

"Hey, it's Aiden."

"Hi, how are you doing? How was the jeep ride around the island?"

"It was okay, but I was worried about you."

I debated how much of the details I should give Aiden, but since he went with me and Antonio to the police station, I figured he was entitled to know what happened earlier that evening.

I recounted what happened at the resort pier and the reason

why *señor Domínguez* tried to kidnap us, but I was interrupted before I finished telling Aiden what happened.

"Wait! *Señor Domínguez* had a gun, and you went towards him anyway?" Aiden's voice grew louder in concern.

"I wanted to wait for the police, but Carlos and Antonio already left to confront him, and when I couldn't see where they were, I felt I didn't have a choice," I explained. I tried not to make my tone defensive because I knew Aiden was worried about me. And looking back, I realized how foolish it was.

"I can see the bind you were in, but still, it was dangerous, and I wish I was there with you," Aiden conceded.

"Thank you," I said. I was thrilled Aiden was so concerned for me, and I smiled to myself while I finished telling him how the police appeared just before the dive shop owner was going to tie me like he did with Carlos and Antonio. I also told him *señor Domínguez* confessed to Carlos and Antonio why he tried to blackmail Antonio even though he knew the dive guide didn't kill Drew.

"Hold on- I'm so confused! Neither Antonio nor *señor Domínguez* killed Drew?" Aiden sputtered.

"Isn't it crazy?" I replied. "We still don't know how Drew died!"

We talked for a while longer, but then the tiredness really hit me. I was talking to Aiden when I yawned in the middle of a sentence.

"I'm so sorry!" I was embarrassed because I didn't want him to think he was boring, but Aiden laughed and said, "It's okay. I know you must be exhausted. I'll let you go, but I was wondering if I could take you to the airport tomorrow?"

"Uh, Carlos is coming by tomorrow to do that. And, what about your *cenote* trip?" I asked. I was really flattered by Aiden's attention, and I hoped he would not be jealous of Carlos.

"Oh yeah, I completely forgot about that!" exclaimed Aiden.

"It's probably a good thing Carlos has already agreed to take you to the airport because I don't want to cancel on Antonio. The poor guy would probably lose it after what Drew did to him," he added. "Promise you'll call me when you get back to California."

I agreed I would call him when I got back to San Francisco. We talked a few minutes more and made plans to have lunch at the *Sushi House* in Japantown when Aiden returned to California.

Chapter Thirty-Seven

"So, what happened to Drew," asked Julia as she gently sat down on the couch after handing me a steaming mug of coffee. It had a faint cinnamon fragrance. I smiled. Julia made the coffee I brought back with me from Cozumel.

"Oohh.. thank you *amiga*!" I said as I eagerly took a sip. I arrived back to San Francisco last night, and I was still jet lagged from arriving home so late. We were sitting on Julia's couch with Grumpy laying down between us with his blanket over his head. It never failed to make me chuckle when he did his blanket trick. With Grumpy snoring loudly between us, I retold my best friend the details that transpired over the past few days.

"It turned out Drew died from nitrogen poisoning," I said. My thoughts went back to the last evening in Cozumel at the resort pier. After the police rescued my friends and I, they let us go after they questioned us about *señor Domínguez*'s motives for taking us captive, but it took another day before the autopsy report came back which revealed the cause of the diver's death. During the layover in Dallas, Carlos called to tell me how Drew had died.

Even though Drew bragged to other divers he had the most air remaining, he actually had far less, and he exacerbated his situation when he didn't give himself enough surface time to release the nitrogen in his blood stream which caused him to get decompression sickness; otherwise known as the bends. Drew probably felt the symptoms, and his irritability towards the others was a sign that something was wrong, but no one picked up on the clue because he was a disagreeable person to begin with. So, when Antonio pushed him during their argument, Drew passed out quickly because he was already suffering from low oxygen.

His death was an accident and had *señor Domínguez* been an experienced scuba diver and had the appropriate training like the rest of the dive masters that worked for his company, he would have recognized some of the symptoms Drew displayed while he was still breathing. It was very unfortunate, and if everyone had acted appropriately, Drew would have gotten the help he needed, and the situation with Antonio and Carlos wouldn't have escalated.

In the end, the Mexican police decided not to charge Carlos or Antonio, and since no one was ultimately hurt, they released *señor Domínguez* after they took his gun and fined him for threatening me and my friends. The police also warned him that if he got in trouble with the law again, he would automatically receive prison time due to his past actions.

However, we found out that *señor Dominguez* left a note and had run off. Apparently, he was still in danger from the people who he owned money to. In the note, *señor Dominguez* apologized for all the bad things he did including blackmailing Antonio.

Even though I did not appreciate the dive shop owner for taking my friends hostage, I felt sorry for him and hoped the people he was running away from did not catch him.

As a result of the owner abandoning his diving operations,

the resort decided to sell the shop and everything in it. It turned out the hotel was a silent partner in the business, and the hotel investors did not want to be associated with a company that someone had died at, especially an American tourist, as it was bad for business.

With the upcoming sale of the dive shop, Carlos and Antonio were let go from their jobs, but this misfortune turned out to be a once in a lifetime opportunity for the two former dive shop employees. They agreed to buy all of the scuba diving equipment and open a dive shop in Tulum where they would offer *cenote* dive tours.

"I thought Antonio didn't have any money," Julia said.

"That's true, but Carlos inherited some money when his parents died and their *taqueria* was sold," I explained.

"I guess *señor Domínguez* blackmailed the wrong person. If he tried to blackmail Carlos instead of Antonio, he could have gotten some money," Julia pointed out. I thought about the observation Julia just made, and I realized that was true. In *señor Domínguez*'s desperate state of mind, he didn't clearly think through his plans.

It seemed everything was going to work out for my friends. Carlos and Antonio wanted me to come to Tulum after they got their dive shop set up. I was excited to try *cenote* diving for the first time. And even though I was happy about my friends' new business venture, I felt bad about what happened to Drew. He was not well liked, but he didn't deserve to die that way. Drew probably acted snarky because it was a defense mechanism to shut people down because he cared too much about being liked. Had he been more laid back and not tried to show off, he would have been more accepted by the other divers. I knew what it felt like to be an outsider, and I vowed if I were in a similar situation again, I would try to be more patient.

My reminiscing about Drew was interrupted when Julia said, "and what about Aiden?"

Thinking about Aiden reminded me of our conversation. "Before I left Cozumel, I promised Aiden I would call him when I arrived in California, so I called him this morning."

"Well, don't keep me hanging!" demanded Julia. She put a hand on my knee to keep me from dashing off.

"He's flying home tonight, but instead of driving down to Mountain View, he is going to get a hotel in San Francisco, and we're going to have lunch tomorrow."

My friend's eyes got really big. "Why don't you invite him as your date to the wedding?" Julia asked extremely proud of her idea.

"Uh, let's see how lunch goes and not jump the gun," I said. Although, I had to admit I was also thinking along the same lines as her. However, I had been in a situation before where I met a guy I thought was interesting, but as I grew to know him better, I realized that he wasn't that great. I didn't want to jinx my date with Aiden, so I vowed to keep my expectations in check.

"Where are you guys meeting?" Julia pressed as she was still not satisfied with my answers.

"We are meeting at the *Sushi House* in Japantown. I found out Aiden had visited Tokyo for a week when he was in Law school for vacation. He enjoyed the food and culture so much he started to learn Japanese, and when he graduated, he took an internship with a Japanese law firm.

"Wow, that's awesome! You finally met a guy that likes to travel and learn languages as much as you do."

"I suppose so, but unlike me, he has a job in the U.S., where I have only worked overseas."

"What difference does that make?" asked Julia.

"I don't know. Maybe not a whole lot. You know, I'm in-between teaching jobs, but more than likely, my next job will be overseas again."

"So..." inquired Julia.

"Well, if things get serious between Aiden and me, and I'm not saying that it will, but if it does, then we'll be in a long-distance relationship, and I don't know if that will work."

"Don't borrow trouble," advised Julia. "If you really like each other, then you will figure it out."

That's true I thought as I looked at my best friend. Although we were the same age, it seemed as though Julia was more mature than I was. Perhaps, it was because she had already found the person she was going to spend the rest of her life with. In any case, I decided to take Julia's advice and not put the cart before the horse as the expression went.

"Alright, I'll get through lunch first," I chuckled.

"You'll be fine," Julia smiled at me in support.

I was getting tired of being grilled, so I tried to distract her from asking more questions about my dating life. "Alright, now that I'm back in town, what do we have left to do for the wedding?" I asked. And, as I hoped, Julia was distracted from asking me more questions about Aiden.

"Well, first we still have to do the final fitting for our dresses..." As Julia listed off the remaining items on her checklist, I thought again about the unusual events that happened over the past week. I met some new dive buddies, helped some friends get out of trouble, and possibly met a new boyfriend. It was definitely strange, but I was also excited for my next dive adventure.

The End

Don't miss the next exciting Claire O' Keefe Mystery

BETRAYAL IN THE BAY

Coming in 2024

Keep reading to enjoy a sample excerpt...

Chapter One

My ears perked up at the laughter floating across the Japanese restaurant. The hairs on my arm tingled as my brain frantically tried to process what I was hearing. What were the odds that I would come across the one person that I didn't want to see in the entire world? The universe was playing an awful trick on me.

I closed my eyes for a brief second hoping that I had imagined the sound. Unfortunately, it wasn't the case.

"Yoo-hoo!" I heard a familiar voice call out from behind me.

No, it can't be! I shook my head to erase the figure that popped into my mind. That sounded like Annisa, and there was no way that she could be here. *There's no way that she could be here to interrupt my lunch date with Aiden.* I tried to reassure myself, but I knew that the voice I heard was real, and it belonged to Annisa Choi, my nemesis and Julia's other best friend.

Aiden lifted his dark eyebrow and gave me a concerned look when he saw that I had stiffened my shoulders and stopped talking to listen to the voice behind me.

"Is something wrong?" he asked as he covered my hand with his. His hand was warm, but it wasn't very soothing.

I didn't answer him. Instead, I swiveled around to observe Annisa approaching our table. As usual, her clothes made a statement. She wore a skintight black mini-dress more appropriate for a nightclub than a restaurant. In addition to her form-fitting dress, her five-inch platform sandals made her tower over the seated dining patrons. Annisa had a wide smile plastered on her face as she weaved her way through the tables and chairs. I felt bad for the ladies whose dates were giving Annisa admiring glances as she strutted by.

I realized that my date might also be checking out Annisa. I turned back around to see if Aiden was looking at me or the woman walking toward us, and I was pleasantly pleased to find that he was looking back at me.

I smiled at his handsome face and said, "Julia's friend is making her way over here." I squeezed his hand back to let him know that everything was okay before I placed both of my hands on my lap. Despite my reassurance, I really wanted to grab the glass of chardonnay in front of me and take a big gulp.

"She looks familiar." Aiden scrunched his eyebrows together to recall where he had seen her before.

"She was in Cozumel with the bachelorette party," I explained. It was strange that I had only met Aiden a few days ago when we both went to the island on vacation because it seemed as though I had known him longer than that. While Aidan and his friend Ryan went to Cozumel to finish their open-water scuba diving certification, I was there to celebrate my best friend Julia's bachelorette party. And, of course, diving was a perk of that trip.

Aiden's eyes lit up in familiarity when he remembered meeting her briefly at the hotel bar. I already knew he had met Annisa previously because Julia told me he left shortly after the ladies arrived.

"Oh yeah…" Aiden's voice faded as Annisa arrived. She was stunning to say the least. Her long, black hair was blown out in soft waves, and the makeup was expertly applied to show off a flawless complexion.

"Claire, what are you doing here?" Annisa asked in the way of a greeting. Her voice was friendly, but her enlarged eyes betrayed her astonishment at seeing me on a date, especially with a man as good-looking as Aiden.

Annisa's surprise turned into amusement as she surveyed my outfit. Her eyes traveled from my hair down to the boots that I was wearing. Her lips curled in a slight smirk.

"I like your boots. Prada?"

Fortunately, I had heard of the name, so I knew she was talking about the designer and not some type of food dish.

"No." I had no idea what brand my boots were. When Julia and I went shopping for clothes to wear on my date with Aiden, I bought the first pair of shoes that looked stylish but more importantly, was comfortable.

I didn't recall the brand name, but I figured the pair of boots were acceptable because there was no way Julia would let me buy anything that wasn't stylish. Being a fashionista, my best friend was up to date on the latest trends. She even nodded in approval when I showed her the boots before I tried them on.

At the time, I was pleased the black knee-high boots complemented the black leggings and the ivory tunic that I had bought to wear.

Now seeing how Annisa was dressed, I thought I was underdressed. *Oh well.* Too late now. I tried to push the comparison aside and cleared my throat.

"I'm having lunch with a friend. Annisa, this is Aiden Filipowski. Aiden, this is Annisa Choi." I briefly made the introductions as I figured they would remember they had already met. At least I knew Aiden remembered her.

Annisa turned and stared at Aiden, trying to place his face.

She twisted her face from side to side a few times before she exclaimed, "I remember now! You were in Cozumel too!" She clapped her hands together. "It's so good to see you again." Annisa let out an amused laugh.

"It's nice to meet you again as well," Aiden replied in his low and smooth voice. I really loved the sound of his voice. It had an air of authority. I'd noticed it when we went with Antonio to the police station in Cozumel. Although Antonio and I were nervous and barely managed to give coherent answers, Aiden talked to the police officers without being intimidated by them.

"So, what are we talking about?" Annisa asked conspiratorially and leaned against the table with her hip.

I didn't want her to join us, but having her continue to stand at the table would draw attention from the other people in the restaurant. She was already blocking the narrow space between our table and the table next to us. The waiter had to go around the other side because there wasn't enough room for him to squeeze the tray through.

I looked at Aiden and raised an eyebrow. Aiden quickly understood that I wanted to know if it was okay for Annisa to join us. He met my questioning look and winked back.

"Would you like to have a seat?" Always courteous, Aiden pulled out a chair.

"Aren't you a gentleman?" She gave him a coquettish smile, sizing him up. I could see the wheels spinning in her head as she wondered what he did for a living and if he was successful.

When she sat down, I said, "Aiden and I were making plans to go scuba diving in Monterey next month."

"Sounds like fun!" With her gaze still locked on Aiden, Annisa added, "I think I will join you guys."

I coughed as I choked on the wine that I just sipped. Aiden and Annisa looked at me.

"Are you okay?" Aiden asked, startled. He was about to

come over and pat my back, but I raised my hand and waved him off.

"I'm so sorry," I mumbled. "Wrong pipe," I said still coughing.

I dabbed my napkin over my lips and took a few moments to gather myself, but I finally said, "I didn't realize you had your open water diving certificate." I knew Annisa didn't, but I wanted to give her a way out of her earlier declaration to join us on the dive.

"What?" Annisa's eyes grew large at my comment. "What's an open water certification?" If it were anyone else, the whole situation would be comical, and I would have made a joke about becoming an instant diver. Instead, I gritted my teeth and explained that you needed to be certified for scuba diving.

"Oh, how silly of me. I thought I could just sign up for the trip." She flipped her hair back over her shoulder and smiled as though it was no big deal.

I gave a weak chuckle as I thought to myself how idiotic the excuse sounded.

"Before you can rent scuba diving equipment, you need to take a two-week course. It's not difficult, but you have to take classroom sessions where you'll read the material and take tests. Then you'll do your practice sessions in the pool before you do your four qualifying dives in the open water. If you pass all that, you'll be certified to dive anywhere in the world." I tried to sum up the training in a nutshell.

"Sounds fascinating," Annisa replied. My eyebrows flew up in surprise because I knew she couldn't possibly be interested in anything that involved getting her hair wet and ruining her hairstyle.

"If you're really interested in scuba diving, we can wait until you get certified to go on the trip," Aiden said. He smiled at me thinking that he solved a problem. He looked proud of himself, and I didn't have the heart to chide him for inviting my frenemy on our next date. I smiled back, but my heart dropped thinking about Annisa joining us on the dive.

"Perfect! I'm sure I can find someone to certify me soon." Annisa responded with all the confidence of someone who was completely clueless about how things worked in the scuba diving world.

I felt bad for whoever her instructor was going to be. They didn't know who they were dealing with. I didn't want to show my reservations, so I smiled.

"Perfect," I echoed and took another drink of my chardonnay. I pasted a smile on my face, but I had a queasy feeling that somehow, things would not go as planned.

Acknowledgments

Thank you Suzanne Meyer and Stephanie Kang for being my super beta readers. Your honest opinions were really helpful, and I couldn't have revised the storyline without your feedback. You guys are the best!

I also want to thank Christine Cover Design for gorgeous book cover.

About the Author

Cindy Quayle is the author of the Claire O'Keefe mysteries. Cindy lives in Fayetteville, Arkansas with her husband, two teenage boys, and two mischievous beagles. Her love for story-telling began when she read *Anne of Green Gables* by Lucy Maud Montgomery in elementary school. Cindy is active on social media as *cqwrites*, and you can follow her for updates on the next Claire O'Keefe mystery.

 instagram.com/cqwrites

 facebook.com/cqwrites

Made in United States
North Haven, CT
01 February 2024

48165713R00148